ONE TO WATCH ME

Book one

ONE World

Alicia Maxwell

Copyright:

Editor/Proofreader: Taryn Lawson
ISBN: 978-0-9992598-0-1 (e-book)
ISBN: 978-0-9992598-2-5 (paperback)
Published by: Alicia Maxwell

About the Author:

Alicia Maxwell is the author of emotionally charged contemporary romance with a suspenseful edge. Her work centers on obsession, deception, and the kind of chemistry that refuses to stay contained.

She is best known for *The ONE Duet—One to Watch Me* and *One to See Me—*a gripping two-book series that blends passion, secrets, and high-stakes relationships.

Writing from South Florida, Alicia brings atmosphere, intensity, and sharp emotional tension into every story she tells.

Dedication:

To my One.
Thank you for believing in me and encouraging me
to take this journey.

Contents

Chapter 1

The plane is accelerating, getting ready to take off the ground. I hear the turbines working, feel my body being pushed into the cushioned seat, and get even more anxious. Flying has never been my thing. No matter how many times I've done it—and we are talking a hundred, no less—I'm a nervous mess every time. Take offs and landings are the worst. I can deal with being up in the sky, the serenity of the view takes my breath away and calms me. The getting to and from that high is a whole different story. Working in my family's investment firm, I endure flying on a weekly basis. Every time, I try to talk myself into not caring about the upcoming flight, only to get on the plane and get anxious all over again. Luckily, I'm taking this trip for pleasure. Should make me feel better, but it doesn't.

Finally, the plane loses contact with the ground and lifts into the air. We are taking off from O'Hare, so it takes a sharp angle up and I grip the armrests, my knuckles white from pressure. Just another few minutes, keep it together a few more minutes and it will get easier. I'm tight, my muscles tense, my nerves in coils. Taking slow, shallow breaths, I try to think of something relaxing. The ocean comes to mind, blue and endless, wave after wave after wave, slow and peaceful. My thoughts drift to my destination: Miami. I'm finally taking the trip I've been planning for a few years—planning, but never actually making. There was always something urgent that required my attention, or the timing wasn't right, or my family had other plans that required my presence.

At last, we reach a high altitude and the plane levels off. I visibly relax and let go of the armrests. I have three hours to spare with no propositions to review or documents to go over: a rare luxury for me. My days are usually planned to the minute, weeks in advance.

I close my eyes and think about my life. After all, this is, for the most part, why I'm taking the trip: to rethink my life, set new priorities, and most importantly, plan a new path.

I'm in my late twenties—a successful young heiress to the family business. I'm good at what I do, and I know it. Years of nonstop work will do that to you.

My family owns a real estate investment and management company. In the years since my graduation, I've initiated and completed several projects, effectively doubling the company's worth by reversing a near-collapse situation and taking advantage of the overall economic downturn. In addition, I've managed to attract a few major investors. I love and hate what I do. I wish I could make my own decisions, bring the company into the twenty-first century. Instead, I feel stuck. My father has little trust in my decisions and ultimately, he maintains tight control of things.

Being a part of the family business is both a blessing

and a curse. I have to fight with my old-fashioned father every step of the way, then never hear one good word once my idea proves to be a success. Even with all the setbacks, I've managed to build quite a reputation in Chicago and beyond its limits, on both coasts. Luckily, I don't conduct any business in Miami yet, so I'm running a small chance of being recognized. Good for me, given the current state of my personal life.

My personal life! That's a different story, one that can hardly be called a success. I used to think I had it all together, completely figured out. Turned out that could not have been further from the truth.

I think back to my first relationship. Stanley was my high school sweetheart. It was four years of pure affection, followed by two more years of unsuccessful attempts to keep us together. We met at the start of freshman year and dated throughout high school. Unfortunately, our relationship did not stand a chance in the real world.   We never survived the long distance after he went away to college. Trying to keep it alive for two years eventually proved to be too hard, and we decided to end things peacefully and promised to stay friends, or as close to it as possible. I felt heartbroken nonetheless, thinking I should've done something differently, put in more effort, maybe even followed him to college. He went to an engineering school, and I was aiming for a business career. Now I realize we were just kids, more friends than lovers for sure.

My second and only other relationship was the serious kind. He was older and wiser. He exuded confidence and respect. We met right after I got my bachelor's degree. I was barely twenty-one, while he was thirty-three. My parents approved, and I even suspected they arranged our meeting. He was a successful businessman and *marriage material*, as my mother put it. I was told to be a good girl and warned not to screw it up.

By the time we met, I'd been single for a year. After a rather busy but lonely year of self-pity and doubt, I was ready to put that chapter of my life behind me. I welcomed the idea of meeting someone new. I was even pleased to have my parents' approval. They never took Stanley seriously, so I felt like a grown-up next to Matthew. I realized, though not soon enough, the choice was taken away from me and they were making the decisions yet again. They had plans for me and Matthew before I ever met him.

My parents have been planning my life since I was a little girl. I never rebelled, justifying it by telling myself that they loved me and wished me the best. All these years I've been living in denial, thinking if my parents thought so highly of my boyfriend, then he *must* be a good person.

Little did I know... He was the exact opposite of what I thought. My parents are still in their own state of denial, thinking it was my fault we didn't work out. They assumed I went away to get a better perspective on my life, so I could come back and fix everything.

The truth is, we haven't had a real relationship in

years. Come to think of it, I don't think passion was ever there at all. Pragmatism is what ruled, from day one. At first, I tried to get him to do fun and romantic things. In return, he would ruthlessly throw it back in my face, telling me I was being childish. I was hurt at first, but then I would end up blaming myself, as I always tend to do. He was older, so maybe I *was* being childish after all. I thought that's what being in an adult relationship must be like. My parents were a lot like Matthew, and they've been married for thirty years.

On the outside, he was the proper, polished version of the perfect life partner: caring, attentive, reliable, cultured—a gentleman in all aspects of the word. On the inside, our relationship was empty. At times, it felt as if he was on autopilot around me, saying what needed to be said, being courteous when necessary, but showing no interest in who I was. At first, I didn't realize any of this; I was too young and busy with school and work. I was too excited to be in a relationship, especially with someone so sophisticated. As the time went by, I realized more and more there was something dysfunctional about us.

Being the gentleman he appeared to be, he proposed right after I finished school. We moved in together shortly thereafter. We had a little family thing going. Once again, everything was picture perfect on the outside. Unfortunately, the more I looked at it, the more I saw him living another life, one that didn't involve me. Once my eyes were wide open, I saw more than I ever could have imagined. Two-faced does not even begin to describe him. Six years of my life wasted. I had been just a career milestone to him.

After we got engaged, my father offered executive positions and stakes in the company to both of us. I wanted to try doing things on my own, but I was again pushed and, as always, I gave in. My parents talked about me being ungrateful for all they'd done for me. The least I could do was work for and help expand the family business. They said it hurt them to think a stranger, meaning my fiancé, was more eager to work for the family business than their own daughter. I felt, yet again, obligated, and ashamed I didn't see it this way myself.

The reality is, I've been living up to someone else's standards my whole life. The harder I worked, the harder I was pushed. I graduated high school having already completed my first year of college, then finished my bachelor's in less than three years. Finally, I got my MBA from Kellogg. Through it all, I was working, interning at the family firm. To say I had no social life is the understatement of the century.

I'm grateful to my parents for giving me the opportunity, but the cost was way too high. I had to grow up all too fast, skipping some of the steps to adulthood completely.

Here I am at twenty-seven, dead tired and totally confused about who I am. I never lived the life of an average teenager or partied my way through college. I feel too old, too serious, and desperate to change something before it's too late.

I'm taking this trip to get away from my reality, to try and be myself without the pressure of expectations. I want to relax and stop looking over my shoulder all the time. I want to have time to meet my own self.

Back in Chicago, people expect me to behave a certain way, to be mature and contained, act with dignity and grace—a shining example of a perfectly raised daughter, top student, aspiring business woman, and heiress. There's no room for anything else, and that's how I've lived my whole life.

Unfortunately, outside of these confines, I don't know who I am. I've yet to start living on *my own*, making *my* mistakes. I need to rethink my life, reset my priorities, free my mind of the constant guilt trip.

I love Miami! It was the first place my thoughts went when I decided to get away. It's so different, so easygoing compared to Chicago. I love that the ocean is endless, and the air is hot and humid. I wanted to enjoy everything, from the sand and the palm trees, to the freedom to be myself. I refuse to be judged by my looks and actions. I've been living up to an image for as long as I can remember. Either I need a break, or I *will* break.

I spend most of the three-hour flight thinking about my life and where I want it to go. I'm conflicted about what exactly I want to achieve by going to Miami. I know I need an outlet, but I'm not used to having days to myself. I had to work hard to clear my schedule for the next three weeks. This is how long I gave myself to relax, rethink my life, and try to determine the path I should follow. It is too ironic to have to reevaluate your whole life in three weeks, having the schedule filled three months in advance. This is the first time I'm going somewhere alone, and by far the most free time I've had in my adult life. You could call me a workaholic, except they usually enjoy what they do; I just do it. It's just business, just obligations.

I tense as the plane starts to descend and grab the armrests all over again. I shut my eyes tight and breathe ever so slowly. Just a few more minutes and I'll be on the ground. The plane makes a rough landing, and I bite my lower lip to fight back the anxiety attack. I gnaw until I can almost taste the coppery blood. The pilot announces our arrival, and I open my eyes. My heart rate is slowing and I take a few full, deep breaths. Finally, I'm safe on the ground.

Chapter 2

Exiting the plane makes me feel tremendously better. Feet firmly on the ground, I follow the instructions around the terminal. First stop, baggage claim. Second stop, rental car office.

This is another exciting part of traveling on my own: I rented an Audi A4 convertible. I'm going to have fun, just like I promised myself. In Chicago, I have a Lexus SUV: luxurious, comfortable, reliable, and *conservative*. The Audi has all the same qualities, but it's sporty and adventurous. Nothing exotic. Keeping a low profile is better in my case. I've been down that road before, where I'm looked at as an asset, a career advancement, a status symbol. I want none of that now. Just the simple me.

I get settled into my new ride and put in the address for the rental condo. Plugging in my iPhone, I go for my playlist. I decide on Maroon 5 mixed with some SHM. I love their track "Don't You Worry Child." Makes me want to believe the heavens really do have a plan for me. The night is warm, and I put the top down. I try not to get lost navigating the ramps around the airport and luckily make it to the highway pretty quickly. Music is blasting from the speakers, and I'm speeding down I-95. The wind is in my hair, whipping it into a crazy mess. The neat waves that once were are long-gone now, replaced by wild and tangled curls. I guess I won't be wasting time straightening my hair on this trip—in a battle with the Miami weather, I didn't stand a chance. On second thought, I kind of like this new, raw look.

Half an hour later, I arrive at the condo. It's a tall, modern, glass building right on the ocean. Palm trees line the front, and the fountain is lit up from beneath the water's surface. I turn the car and luggage over to the valet, grab my purse, and enter the foie. The interior is luxurious, with ceilings three stories high and intricate granite patterns on the floor. There are antique-looking columns scattered all around, and arches leading down to secluded alcoves stuffed with seating areas. The whole place is a mix of European luxury and tropical comfort. A bar is tucked away in the far corner, private and inviting.

A tall blond with a professional smile plastered on her face greets me from behind a rich mahogany concierge desk covered in black granite. I make quick work of checking in, then head for the elevators. I rented a one-bedroom apartment with a full kitchen, living room, and a separate master bedroom suite. Once upstairs, I slide the key card into the lock and push the door open.

What I see is everything I wished for, plus a little more. The foie area is covered in white stone tile brushed to a mirror shine. To the right is the living area, with an open gourmet kitchen. The cabinets are white and glass, with some built-in lights to make everything glow. The countertops are charcoal grey, with sparkles twinkling from somewhere deep in the stone. The kitchen itself is a work of art, and I promise myself I'll take full advantage of it.

I make my way down to the living room. The entire back wall is made of glass, with a sliding door leading to a wide balcony. The moonlight is reflected in the ocean, and I see the white foam of the waves breaking against the shore. It's late, past eleven for sure, but below me, life is raging.

Walking around the dinette set, I see a recliner covered with a luxurious pillow top and towels, then spot another sliding door leading to the bedroom. In the center is a king-sized bed, positioned for a view of the ocean. The headboard is a mix of dark wood and lush, soft fabric; beige, brown, and teal patterns echo the colors of the beach and the ocean. There are at least fifteen throw pillows, all different shapes and sizes, sitting at the header. I sprint a few steps forward and jump onto the bed. I laugh to myself, happy as a kid. I love it!

Finally, I make my way to the bathroom, and oh my, oh my! It's huge! There is a Jacuzzi tub that could easily fit two, a stone-walled shower with multiple jets lining the walls, and two sinks with at least four feet of gorgeous marble counter space between them.

Everything is covered in light beige stone with golden undertones. I can almost see my own reflection in every shining surface. This is simply amazing! I can't say I haven't stayed in nice places before, but this place makes me feel something different. It's probably the fact that I'm alone here. This is my own little fairy tale.

I look into the mirror and see myself smiling; even my eyes have a new sparkle to them. I'm normally a composed person, with a polite smile that rarely touches my eyes. I look closer and see evidence of my recent lack of sleep, in the form of new under-eye circles. I look a little paler too. No wonder, I never had any dinner. Food and flying are a bad combination for me.

I decide to unpack, take a quick shower, and head to bed. I finish everything in under an hour and climb the pillows to get under the covers. The bed feels like a cloud, and sleep takes me in minutes.

Chapter 3

The first rays of the rising morning sun brighten the room, and I peel open my eyes. It's early—the sun is still climbing—but I'm brimming with energy. This is the first time in months I've woken up looking forward to the day. I feel energized, despite getting just five hours of sleep, at best.

I decide to start the day, even though I could probably sleep till noon and no one would care. Getting out of bed, I take in my ocean view then head straight for the balcony. The horizon line looks stunning through the floor-to-ceiling windows, but outside, it's simply breathtaking.

The beach seems deserted and there aren't many cars on the streets yet. I ignore the fact that I'm dressed only in a white, see-through camisole that barely reaches my thighs and step out onto the balcony. The salty ocean breeze gently caresses my bare skin, and I feel the sun's warm rays kissing my arms, shoulders, and face. Long curls graze my cheeks, and I lift them up and away from my face and neck. I close my eyes and take a deep breath. I can hear the waves breaking against the sand, and I feel lightweight, almost ready to fly. This is heaven! I open my eyes and take it all in: the beach, the ocean, the breeze. I inhale deeply, and the briny scent of seaweed reaches my nostrils; the morning tide brought slick green clumps of it ashore.

I look around. My condo is on the twentieth floor—not *too* high, by Miami high-rise standards, but high enough for a good view. On my right are the ocean and the beach, and on my left is Collins Avenue, the artery spanning the peninsula from South Beach all the way north, to Hollywood. In front of me is a tall building with amazing glass walls that serve as floor-to-ceiling windows. It's so early, I don't see a single person on the balconies. The city is still asleep.

The wind blows a little harder and the hem of my camisole flies up and bares my butt. I instinctively grab it and pull down. I feel the pink creeping into my cheeks, but I remind myself there's no reason to be shy. I'm all alone here. And then I decide on a bold move. In a single, swift motion, I raise the hem over my head and take off the cami. I'm a grown woman, after all, and I can tan topless if I want to... Even if I do feel a bit self-conscious about it. I would probably never dare to do this on an actual beach, but here, twenty stories high, in the privacy of my own balcony and with no one around, I try to leave my inhibitions behind. I lower down onto a chaise lounge covered in the softest pillows and cotton towels, and stretch myself out to tan my skin. Closing my eyes, I relax and let the sun caress my body. The breeze covers my skin in goosebumps and my nipples become hard. I feel aroused without even being touched. I try to remember the last time I had sex, but it only stirs up the painful memories.

I try to think of something tranquil, like the seagulls flying above the water, or the palm trees lining the beach—whatever it takes to calm down and avoid touching myself. I feel my skin getting warm under the sun and realize I probably need some sunblock. I take the bottle of lotion from the cocktail table by my side and squirt some into my palm, rubbing my hands together to spread it. I lift my right leg in the air and begin at my ankle, going up to the knee and then back, making sure to cover the front and back, then repeating the same procedure on the left leg. Then I get a little more lotion and start working from my knees up to my lacy bikini. The trick is to stay on my legs and not wander off. I feel the lace getting wet from my arousal. I'm moving to my stomach now, and it's also time to cover my breasts in their protective layer of sunblock. I squirt a good amount into my hand and start working circles around my hips and ribs, up to the swell of my chest. I am aching so badly at my core, it feels almost *too* dangerous to touch my nipples. I cup my breasts with my hands and lather lotion all around them, reaching to my collar bone and shoulders. I only have to finish my arms and whatever I can reach of my back, and I'm good to go. I wrap things up and relax back on the chaise.

I can't concentrate on anything, so I decide to focus on my breathing. I start thinking of the yoga classes I used to take in Chicago and inhale deep breaths in and out. I lose my senses of time and place, and feel like I'm floating in the ocean breeze. At some point, I realize the real world around me is waking up, as cars trickle onto the streets, and the hum of life below grows louder.

* * *

I see her.

I check the watch on my wrist automatically. It's early. She stands by the rail, seemingly enjoying herself.

I aim my optics, just for kicks. She surely deserves a closer look.

Just as I set the lens in place, she moves. The next moment, my eyes catch her. She is naked, sans the scrap of lace covering her pussy.

I watch her freely, knowing I am invisible.

This is an unanticipated turn of events. I laugh at my raging hard-on and the unexpected cause of it.

I don't need this distraction now. I need to focus.

* * *

Standing up, I look around. The scenery is about the same as it was, except there are more people milling about on the ground now. The balconies of the building across from mine are empty. Somehow, I have the nagging feeling I'm being watched. It's probably my self-consciousness talking, making me feel guilty about the topless tanning. I ignore the little voice in my head and decide it's time to finish up my nude yoga/sunbathing session. I'm calmer now, but a good run along the beach would definitely finish clearing my mind. Inside, I change into a sporty bikini. I'm not a big girl, but I do have some curves to show. My breasts are not small by any means, and I usually pick sports bras with good support. I hate to have them jiggling all around when I run. I add a long, white linen shirt on top and button it in the middle. Then I freshen up in the bathroom, apply more sunblock to my face, and grab the beach bag, my sunglasses, keys, and a towel. I go out onto the balcony one more time and take a look at the beach below. It's still pretty deserted, save for the occasional runner here and there.

I decide to go running barefoot along the water. With the beach service still closed at this early hour, I leave my things behind on the sand. The waves bring the warm water to my feet and I start stretching. I bend down and hug my ankles, one at a time, then rise to my tip-toes and stretch my arms up and out. A few minutes later, I'm ready to run. I choose to go right, heading south from my building. The sun is on my left, and I'm trying to keep looking at the ocean without being

25

blinded. I start slowly, but soon enough, I'm running at full speed, bringing my knees and hips forward with each step.

I run freely, remembering what it felt like to be a teenager. Even then, I found peace in running. I would run a few miles at a time, just to clear my mind. Years later, it still works. I feel a pleasant burning in my muscles and keep going forward.

I pass a newly restored fishing pier. The old one was destroyed by a hurricane a few years back. I continue running, making a mental note to come check out the renovations. There's also a bar there now, one that should offer a breathtaking view of the skyline.

Once I reach the last tall building, I turn around and head back. I notice a guy running past me farther down south. He is tall and well-built, moderately tan. He's wearing a pair of wrap-around sunglasses, but he passes by too quickly for me to get a good look at his face. I watch his figure accelerating away from me, then switch my attention back to running. Interesting, I hadn't noticed him, although he must have been right behind me.

The run back is harder than I expected. The sun climbs, and the air grows hot and humid. I run slower and really push myself the last quarter mile, making a mental note to pace myself better next time.

Completely exhausted, I wave the beach service guy to get me a chair and umbrella while I jump into the water. The waves hit my boiling body with an icy grip. I must have overheated. Running by the water, my feet got accustomed to its temperature, while my body stayed hot. The contrast of the cold water against my hot skin makes my chest tighten from the lack of oxygen. I swim a few strokes and try to normalize my breathing. I do not risk going in deep, and instead stay in the shallow spot where I can safely stand above the waves. I run my palms over my face, washing away the heat and sweat. Moments later, I'm out of the water and dragging back to my now-set-up chair and umbrella. I drop down and completely relax every muscle in my body. Closing my eyes, I just lie there and breathe. Running and swimming left me exhausted, and I drift away.

* * *

I see her.

She looks edible in her bikini, running along the shore.

Hot and sweaty, just like I'd like to make her.

She lays down, all on display, as if inviting me for a view.

Focus, man, focus.

Chapter 4

I wake suddenly with the feeling I'm being watched. A quick look around leaves me feeling dizzy, yet reveals no possible stalker. People around me seem completely oblivious to my existence. As I lie back down, I wonder why I'd suddenly felt eyes on me. My head is still spinning, while my body feels hot. Falling asleep in the shade, I managed to wake up in the sun. The sun must have moved. I touch my sensitive skin and realize I've probably burned. Should have put on sunblock before passing out.

Now seems like a good time to call it a day and go back into the comfort of the air conditioner, maybe take a cool bath. As I gather my things, the beach service guy who set me up in the morning comes by. Realizing I never thanked him for the chairs, I dig through my bag in search of a few bucks.

"Thank you for chairs and towels. I was too exhausted after my run and completely passed out."

His smile is genuinely friendly. "Not a problem, miss. It's my pleasure."

I smile back. This guy seems really nice, and he's rather cute. Too young though. I bet young girls ask him for help applying sunblock all the time. Oh, what am I thinking? I've got to turn down the vacation mode.

"I'll be back tomorrow morning."

He smiles again. "I'll take care of you. Just let me know if you need anything. How long are you staying with us, miss?" Is it me, or did he smile wider at the word *anything*? Oh god, I've definitely got to stop. He is seriously young.

"I should be here for three weeks."

"Great, I'll see you tomorrow then. I'm Adrian by the way." He extends his arm and I shake it automatically in a greeting.

"Nice to meet you, Adrian. I'm Emmeline."

"Great! Enjoy your stay."

"See you tomorrow! And thanks again!"

As I leave, I see Adrian making his way to another umbrella, greeting a leggy brunette. His smile is as genuine as before. I wonder if he truly enjoys his job, being surrounded by new people all the time. Or maybe it's the ease of vacation that keeps these ladies relaxed and flirty. Either way, I almost envy him for doing something he enjoys so much every day.

As soon as I step foot inside the building, the cold, air-conditioned air attacks me. My skin is covered in goosebumps, and the wait for the elevator seems like an eternity. My nipples get tight and peak through the swimsuit, leaving me feeling self-conscious. I cross my arms over my chest, only to expose my cleavage instead. A few people are gathered around, waiting for the elevator, exchanging looks. Finally, the elevator makes it down to the beach level and I step inside. A moment later, I'm exiting on the twentieth floor. The hallway here is as frigid as it is downstairs, and I make a mental note to buy myself a fluffy cotton beach wrap, preferably one with a hood.

Inside, my condo is as freezing as the rest of the building. I open the balcony door to let in the warm air and get into the shower. The water is nice and hot and I enjoy the warmth, only to be immediately assaulted with a burning feeling and chills over my body. This is weird! Then it dawns on me: I burned, so I'm hot and cold all at once. And on the first day of my vacation—lucky me. Now I'll have to avoid the sun for a few days. I guess Adrian won't get a chance to take care of me tomorrow after all.

I get dressed and close the balcony doors. The rooms are warm and humid. I step out to the balcony and admire the view. The beach is filled with people in the water and on the sand. What was a deserted, serene place just hours ago is bursting with activity now. Collins Ave is filled with traffic. The plazas across the street are overflowing with cars and people. I decide to take a walk and get some lunch in one of the cafes.

The lobby is, not surprisingly, frigid as well, while the outside is hotter than the balcony. It's too hot for a walk, so I take my car and just drive around.

Several cute restaurants and cafes with inviting tables are scattered along the plaza. My lunch is a freshly squeezed juice and a salad. It's hard to eat when it's so hot.

Looking around, I find a yoga place and decide to try it out tomorrow. Being a big fan, I usually try to go at least a few nights each week in Chicago. Finding one so close by here is super exciting.

The next destination is a shopping mall. My vacation wardrobe needs to be updated and expanded. As much as I enjoy shopping, I'm usually rushing through it. Today's objective is to take time and enjoy. And so I do. I choose the Bal Harbour Shops, a place conveniently close by, and with outdoor terraces, rather than freezing indoor hallways. I've been there a few times on my previous stays in Miami and liked it a lot. It's on the upper end, but totally worth the trip. Besides the traditional upscale brands, it houses some rare ones as well. I walk around window shopping first. My organizational skills kick in even while I shop. Once I see the boutiques I'm interested in, I start going in.

I find one, full of linen tops and dresses. Several things, coincidentally all white, fit very well and end up in the shopping bag. Then, I stop by a couple more places and opt for a selection of white and off-white pieces. It feels liberating to get out of the business suit and into free-flowing, white, summer things.

On my way out I spot the La Perla boutique, turn the

corner, and walk in. The amount of lace and sexuality overwhelms me. This place is heaven on Earth. I am immediately greeted by a middle-aged woman who reminds me of my French tutor. I don't even know why I'm here. I have plenty of underwear, and I'm all alone, with no romantic plans. Yet, I'm here and I want new lingerie. It will be a symbol of a fresh start, a new me. I tell the sales representative that I want to replace my existing collection with a new one. Her reserved look is shaken for a second and her eyes light up with excitement. I figure she must be making a great deal in commissions here, but she also, somehow, looks genuinely happy. I wonder how often she gets ladies in here that are making a new start. She must see right through me. Being a professional salesperson, she stays on the subject at hand, never veering into personal territory.

We talk about styles while roaming around the floor exploring different models and colors. I point to the ones I like and she nods in agreement, as if memorizing my choices. When we're done, I step into the dressing room and start trying on endless ensembles of bras and panties, bustier and garter belts, silk camisoles and robes. I love most of the pieces and soon enough, the stack grows to a considerable height. I can't even imagine how much it would cost. I've never spent so much on lingerie in my life. Sorting through the pile, I realize once again I love them all. Oh my god! Sexy does not begin to describe it. These garments are so sensual, I wish I had someone to appreciate them with.

One hour and a capital X number of dollars later, I

leave La Perla feeling ready to conquer the world in my new lingerie. I have done more shopping in one day than I have in months. I think there must be something to the cliché about women and shopping; it does put me in a better mood. My next stop is a cute cafe upstairs. I choose an out-of-the-way corner featuring a casual, antique-looking couch and a coffee table. Settling in with my bags, I take a look at the menu and notice some interesting offerings. I decide to go with an iced espresso drink infused with liqueur and a selection of macaroons in exotic flavors. Should be interesting.

The minute I raise my eyes from the menu in search of the waiter he seems to materialize out of thin air. I smile, feeling a little startled, and place my order.

I am not used to going out alone, so for lack of anything better to do I grab my smartphone and start checking email. Being a weekend, there are barely any new work-related emails. In minutes I'm out of reading material. Spotting a stack of newspapers and magazines laying conveniently on the side, I look through them and grab one.

Wow, being in public alone is weirder than I thought. Usually I'm in such a rush to get through my lunch that I barely notice it, but now, having just a coffee, it feels too lonely.

I think back to what I left in Chicago: the life I had, or thought I had. There is no way I'm going back to Matthew. I'll have to start all over. Maybe it's not such a bad thing after all. As the saying goes, whatever happens, happens for the best.

My thoughts are interrupted. A man is standing next to my table, and I look up at him without registering what he is saying. He looks at me as if expecting an answer, and I realize he was talking to me. I guess I was too deep in thought. I blush slightly.

"I'm sorry, what did you say?" He tilts his head, smiling at me.

"I was wondering if this seat was taken."

I look around, trying to see if there are any open tables, and notice the cafe is completely full. When did that happen? Must be lunchtime, or some five o'clock tea time around here. It was rather quiet just minutes ago. So the guy is not openly hitting on me, probably just wants to sit down. I point to the seat across the table.

"Of course, please!"

Instead, he lowers himself down onto the other side of my love seat, completely ignoring the chair on the opposite side. I reconsider whether he's hitting on me.

I'm so used to being *with someone, in a relationship, or engaged* that I subconsciously reject any advances in my direction. But I'm single now, single! I guess it will take some time to get used to.

I see the menu by my side and hand it to the stranger.

"Here, you might want to take a look." I smile and watch him. He takes the menu and our fingers brush for a mere fraction of a second. I look up at his face, and really look at him this time. He's wearing a pair of wrap-around sunglasses that shield his eyes completely. His face is tan, covered in a typical Armani-style stubble. Strong cheek bones, full lips, and a straight Roman nose finish the look. Something about him seems very familiar. He busies himself checking out the menu, and I take a moment to study him further. His hair is light brown with occasional dirty blond locks, probably burned by the sun. It's wavy and messy. He is dressed in a light beige shirt with the sleeves rolled up, revealing his muscular forearms. Jeans tightly hug his thighs, and a rather prominent bulge. My eyes don't linger there too long, for fear of being caught.

He seems young, but I can't tell how young. The shades cover too much, and I wish he had removed them. I doubt that would be happening—we are sitting outside, and the sun is merciless. I realize my face is equally hidden by my huge Diors, an advantage when it comes to checking him out.

I look away just in time to avoid being caught ogling him. How lucky!
The waiter materializes again, and I wonder if he's somewhere spying on patrons—this cannot be pure coincidence.

My new tablemate places his order for some southern variation of an espresso drink and turns to face me. The top few buttons of his shirt are open, giving a sneak peek of his tan chest, and I wonder what it looks like bare. It must be spectacular and built, firm and tan. Wow, where did that come from? I look away and try not to blush again. Oh my, this is embarrassing. Thank god for the shades, at least they half-cover my face and blushing cheeks.

"Let me introduce myself, I'm Alex." I extend my arm for a handshake.

"I'm Emmeline." He takes my hand in his, slowly turns it, and places a soft kiss that wakes a flurry of butterflies in my stomach.

"It's a pleasure to meet you Emmeline."

I immediately love the way he pronounces my name. He has the slightest British accent, mixed with something else. I cannot quite place it, but it is sexy as hell. His voice is deep, yet soft, with silvery undertones.
My hand is still in his, and I feel reluctant to break contact.

"I see you've been shopping." He points to the pile of shopping bags in the corner and I nod. My La Perla bag sits prominently on top.

"Yes, guilty as charged." I smile and wonder if he noticed what exactly I've been shopping for.

"Most guys hate taking women shopping, I actually find it rather amusing. If you do it right, it's like watching a kid on a Christmas morning, plus you get a fashion show out of it. I would have loved to see you trying those on." He chuckles, and I know he means the lingerie.

"I guess you would, wouldn't you? Too bad I'm done." I giggle and smile at him. Two can play this game.

"Are you here to shop?" I ask. He looks at me, amused, and smiles.

"Yes, indeed. Did you want to see the fashion show?"

"That depends on what you'd be shopping for."

"Does it now?" He gives me a one-sided smile, and I melt. I guess it does not, but I'm not telling him that. In truth, how often does one get to see a hot guy trying on clothes? Exactly! But this hot guy is a stranger I just met, so this would be highly inappropriate.

We are interrupted by the waiter placing our drinks on the table.

"Allow me." Alex says, reaching for my glass and handing it to me. Our fingers brush again and I feel the butterflies in my stomach coming alive. I haven't had such a reaction to a guy's touch since I was a teen, and even then, it was different.

We spend the next half hour talking about everything and nothing. It's fun and easygoing; we steer clear of talk of personal things. At the end, all I've learned about him is his name. I'm not sure about him, but as for me, meeting new people is still awkward. Although I'm single, I have a hard time wrapping my head around it. Besides, I'm trying to keep a low profile here.

"Well, I better go, I still need to unpack and try everything on." I joke, pointing at my pile of shopping bags.

"You wouldn't want to miss that. I know I wouldn't for sure!" We both laugh. Alex gets up to his feet, throws a few bills on the table and extends his arm to help me off the couch. He raises my hand to his lips and kisses my knuckles again.

"It was a pleasure meeting you, Emmeline. If you need company for your fashion show, keep me in mind. I promise to be honest and objective!" Just for a second I imagine him watching me and immediately feel my nipples tightening with arousal.

"Maybe next time," I laugh, to avoid looking flustered.

"Then, there will definitely be a next time," he says, the confidence in his voice leaving no doubt. It would be a lie to say I'm not looking forward to it.

Gathering my bags, I try to step between people and tables without knocking anything down. Alex gets a hold of the whole bunch in one swift motion, and raises them high above us with one hand, while putting his other at the small of my back and guiding me out. My skin feels hot under his touch, and I almost want to slow down and enjoy it a moment longer. We pass the tables and I stop to turn around and thank him. As I turn, I bump into his chest and his smell invades my nostrils. He smells of some cologne that I can't place but really enjoy. It's masculine, yet lightly fresh. Alex looks down as I look up and our faces are just inches apart. I am frozen, mesmerized by his proximity, and he doesn't move either. Finally, I step back and look down then back up at him. What if I kissed him now? What if I asked for his number? What if? But instead I extend my hand, palm up, to get my bags back. He keeps them by his side.

"Where are you parked, I'll walk you to your car?"

"I'm on the second floor, but you don't have to do that. I'm a big girl, you know."

"I'm sure you are. Lead the way!" He places his hand at the small of my back and leads me around people and columns. It seems he has no doubt about where to find my car. I feel small next to his large frame, and enjoy the contact his hand is making with my body. We move in unison, reminding me of the ballroom dance classes I took as a child.

"Are you parked somewhere here as well?"

"Yes, I think we are actually in the same lot."

We make it to my car and I open the trunk to load everything.

"Fun car, isn't it?" he asks.

"Oh yes, I love it!" My voice is full of excitement and met by one of Alex's trademark, lopsided smiles.

He opens my driver's door, and I'm caught between him and the car. Our bodies are so close that the smallest movement will put us contact. My eyes are level with his tan chest, peeking out through the open top buttons of his shirt. His unique scent invades my senses, and I want to inhale him as deeply as I can, and nuzzle my face in the crook of his neck. Instead, I'm only capable of taking a shallow breath and trying to control the moan that was about to escape my mouth. Slowly, looking up, I see my own reflection in his sunglasses. He lowers his face and his cheek brushes against mine, stubble gently scraping my skin. Goosebumps spread all over my body. Then his lips touch me in the gentlest kiss right along my jaw line, and I feel his exhale of hot air against my skin. He must have been holding his breath, same as I did. I melt against his touch just for second, pleasure surging through my body and culminating in my core. I wish I could run my hands against his tan chest, kiss my way up his neck to his sensual lips, get lost in the kiss. My thoughts are invaded by a raspy whisper in my ear.

"Till next time, Eline. I will see you soon." Another brush of his unshaven cheek against mine and he straightens and steps away.

My world immediately lacks his scent and touch. His sudden retreat nearly throws me off balance. A tan, muscular arm is on my elbow, righting my stance.

"Till next time." I try my hardest to look unaffected by him as I turn and get behind the wheel.

In seconds, I start the car and open the roof. Alex is standing a few steps away now, giving me room to back out of the spot. I can't tell what he's thinking, his eyes are still shielded by the sunglasses. The last I see of him is in the rearview mirror before I make a turn and lose sight of him.

The road leads to Collins Avenue, and I turn left to go north. What was that just now? I'm trying to process the last hour in my mind, and I'm having a hard time doing it. The way he said my name when he kissed me on the cheek and whispered in my ear, it was so unlike anything I'm used to. My parents prefer Emily, so by default, that's what I go by if I'm not addressed by my full name. I like Eline better, especially the way Alex said it, with his accent.

So I met a guy, a nice and sexy one. We spent an hour together, but somehow it feels as if he knows me more than I know him. Why haven't I gotten his number, or given him mine? He never asked, that's why! But then he insisted on seeing me again, and it looked like he meant it. My head is swimming with questions. When it comes to dating guys, and flirting in general, I'm so out of practice.

What if he asked more questions? I would hate to go into details about the long, disastrous relationship I'm coming out of. Who'd want to hear about that? No one! Especially no one interested in a short-lived vacation fling. I need to put aside all this personal business about coming here to find myself. I've got to start thinking more positively! I've had a great day, and I don't want to spoil it now.

Ten minutes later, I get to my building and give the car to the valet. Once upstairs, the unpacking begins. The clothes are hung in the closet, lingerie put away in the dresser drawers. Everything is organized and it's not even 5 p.m.

What should I do? It's so weird to have these days to myself, with no one to talk to. I change into a pair of linen shorts and a lacy top and decide to go for a walk along the beach. The sun is already setting and the sky is beautiful. It's pink and purple all at once.

Chapter 5

The sand feels so warm and soft under my feet. I wiggle my toes and dig into it a little deeper while contemplating where to go. To my right is the new fishing pier, the one I passed on my run this morning. The whole shoreline should be visible from there, and it will be just gorgeous.
Walking by the water, I'm holding my flip-flops in one hand and picking up seashells with the other. Soon my palm is full, and I have nowhere to put them. Next time I'll bring a bag.

Memories of myself as a little girl surface. Picking sea shells, building castles in the sand, playing in the waves. Those were great and uncomplicated times. I spent a lot of vacations by the ocean, and fell in love with it.

On occasion, I feel as if someone is watching me. Looking around, I see random people, yet no one familiar, or even remotely interested in me.

The pier is lined with benches facing both ways. Settling down to look north, I really begin to admire the view. The skyline is indeed breathtaking from here. New buildings have been popping up over the past few years and there are barely any empty lots left between them. An hour or so passes by unnoticed. Next thing I know, the sun has set, and the buildings are all lit up. Looking back the way I came, I'm debating if I should walk back along the shore, or go grab something to eat first. Some food would be great; my stomach is rumbling.

On the other side of Collins, at 163rd, I find a cozy cafe with an outdoor terrace. Perfect choice! It's a self-service Mediterranean place with an extensive list of salads and sandwiches. I'm starving, and the aroma inside drives me crazy. Finally, I get my tray and settle down on the outside terrace. Either I'm too hungry, or I'm getting better at these lonely meals.

The walk back home along Collins takes about half an hour. As tempting as watching the moon over the ocean sounds, I am not walking the dark beach alone. Moving at half my normal speed, I'm looking around, learning my surroundings. Occasionally, I have the same feeling: the feeling someone is watching me. I think I'm becoming paranoid.

Once home, I take a long, relaxing bath, turning on the jets in the Jacuzzi. The streams of water massage my back and shoulders in a relaxing way. I close my eyes and see Alex's face, feel his touch, his feather-light kiss on my cheek and a raspy voice in my ear: "Till next time, Eline. I will see you soon." Goosebumps run across my body all over again, my nipples becoming tight. I run my palms over my neck, shoulders, and breasts, going to the sensitive area right under them. I'm craving a touch. I lightly pinch and twist one nipple with two fingers, pleasure shooting straight to my core. My other arm works its way down the flat surface of my stomach and lower. I go straight to my sensitive nub and feel it slick with my arousal, even in the water. My fingers circle a familiar pattern and in seconds the coils inside are tightening. I close my eyes and see Alex's lopsided smile, his lips moving as he speaks, a glimpse of his tan chest showing through an unbuttoned shirt. I want to slow down, prolong the pleasure, but I'm just too turned on. I feel the first wave of orgasm sweeping over me and go under. Slowing down the run of circles my fingers are doing around my clit, I plunge two in and curl them to reach the sweet spot inside. I'm gasping for air, moaning, and going through another wave of orgasm. As it wears down, I slowly pull my fingers out and run them lazily up and down across my slit. This was intense. I guess a good fantasy can go a long way.

My body feels deliciously relaxed and tired all at once. I get out and wrap myself in the softest towel, still feeling sensitive. The air-conditioned bedroom feels too chilly, so I go to the terrace. Settling down in the lounge chair, I lay back and relax.

It's dark, and the full moon is hanging low over the ocean. The white foam forming at the tops of the waves looks silvery in its light. Wave after wave crushes against the sand. The sound is lulling me to sleep. The breeze blows over the exposed parts of my body, caressing the warm skin. At some point, I drift off to sleep. Waking up from the chill of the night, I make my way to the huge, king-size bed. I slide the door closed, but I'm just too tired to care about closing the curtains or turning off the night light. I climb under the covers and fall asleep immediately.

* * *

I watch her.

Back on her terrace, in the same spot, sleeping, as if she has not a worry in the world.

I pull away and get back to business.

My eyes wander to her delicious body from time to time.

I don't touch the optics. They put her too close.

I need the distance. I need my focus back.

* * *

I wake up disoriented. It's dark outside. Wondering how long I've slept, I check the clock. It shows 10 a.m. The horizon line is blurred and everything is gray and gloomy. Tropical storms are no fun. In fact, this one lasts all day, and I stay in reading a book. I'm so lazy that I order room service throughout the day and never leave my condo.

Thankfully, the wind is blowing the rain drops away from the rails and I can stay out on the balcony. The city is half asleep, no pedestrians in sight, empty beaches, fewer cars. Even the air smells differently, the scent of the ocean more prominent. The day goes by slowly, but I enjoy it nonetheless.

Going to bed early, I hope for better weather tomorrow.

Chapter 6

The morning sun is in my face and I open my eyes to greet the day. There is no sign of yesterday's storm. The clock on the nightstand is showing 7 a.m. That's 6 a.m. Chicago time—not bad for vacation. I get up to check the weather outside. It's warm, but not hot yet, perfect for a morning run. I stay on the balcony for a few minutes, truly admiring the view and serenity of the city still asleep.

Then I realize the sun will be fully up soon and hurry inside. Minutes later I'm ready and head down to the beach. I leave my things on the sand and start stretching. This time I decide to run north, to the left of my building, starting slowly and working up the speed as I go.
I love it! I lose myself in running, just concentrating on my moves and breathing. The warm ocean water is at my feet and I run ahead, one foot in front of the other, free as a seagull.

At some point, I look to my left and there are no more tall buildings along the beach, just private homes. I must have run far enough to get to the Golden Beach. I slow down to look around. When I look back the way I came, I see a guy running my way, still quite far away. Something about him looks extremely familiar.

I stop to catch my breath, look around, and spot a pretty shell. Bending down, I pick it up, then a few more. I'm always on the hunt for beautiful ones. The beach seems littered with them after the storm. In the few minutes I've been busy collecting my trophies, the man has caught up with me. Turning back, I take a good look, only to realize it's Alex. My heart skips a beat. I'm surprised and beyond delighted. I'm not sure if this is a coincidence or something planned, but I really don't care at the moment.

I take a look at him from top to bottom, thanking my shades for covering my eyes. Hopefully he can't detect my eye movement, and won't catch me ogling him. What I see is beyond pleasant. He is about six-foot-something and well-built, solid, with defined muscles, not over-bulging, just perfect. His abs are well-defined too, a sharp V at the border of trunks that hang dangerously low, especially since he's running. He's got a deliciously tan body and his hair is a wild mess of chocolate brown with an occasional dirty blond wave. His eyes are covered by the black shades of his wraparound sunglasses. I can't see where he is looking, but I can feel his eyes on me. My cheeks are hot and pink from running, but I feel them getting even more flushed. I am not used to being this underdressed and stared at all at once. I lick my lips as I contemplate what to say.

"Hello Eline!" he says, giving me an intriguing smile.

"Hello Alex! Having a good run?" I ask, while I wonder how long he'd been following me.

"Indeed," he smiles. "The views here are amazing." His trademark smile suggests a double meaning. I can't help but wonder if he was smirking at me, or if this is just my self-consciousness talking. I'll bet he was referring to watching my butt all the way up here.

"So I guess you did see me around." I extend my hand and wave it around. He steps closer, takes my hand in his and placing a soft kiss on my knuckles. A jolt of electricity hits my body, and I flinch the slightest bit. He seems to take note of that as well. I can see it in his smile; it deepens on one side. The corner of his mouth is raised, as if he finds it amusing to have such an effect on me. He speaks again, and his voice soft and sexy.

"I promised you would see me again, Eline." So confident, and not a bit ashamed of following me.

I feel his gentle touch as he runs his thumb over my knuckles, and it sends another jolt of electricity through my body that culminates in my core. I inhale sharply and realize he's watching me. I try to exhale as slowly as possible so he wouldn't notice my reaction to his touch, but it seems nothing escapes his attention. He chuckles softly, and that's when I realize my hand is still in his. His touch is gentle and comforting, and he seems to have no intention of letting go.

I'm dying to see his eyes, to get a bit of insight into what he's thinking, but the damn wraparounds hide them completely.

Debating if I should claim my hand back or let him hold it, I decide on the latter. It feels too good to let go. This is so not like me.

51

"Well, this was a nice run. Would you like to take a walk with me back? Care for swim first?" He smiles and asks casually.

I feel drawn to him, as if by magnet, and before I even have time to consider anything, I nod and agree. I'm still at a loss for words, just looking at him and smiling a full-on smile.

"So which one is it? Swim or walk?"

I blink, still mesmerized by this beautiful man standing next to me.

"Ok, then swim it is!" He grabs my hand tightly and pulls me forward before even finishing his sentence.

"Let's go!" He drags me towards the water and the next thing I know, I'm waist-deep in the ocean, the waves crashing at us. The cold water hits my hot skin and I gasp, my lungs filling with air. A strong wave hits us at the same time and I would have fallen, were it not for his strong arms catching me and lifting me to his chest. I look up to his chiseled chin and slightly opened mouth covered in drops of water. The thought runs through my mind: I want to kiss him.

I slide down his body and he puts me back on my feet.

"Ok there?"

"Yes, thank you for catching me."

"Any time, you're a nice catch," he says, the corner of his mouth curving up again.

"Ha-ha, very funny! I guess I walked right into that one. I could have fallen, you know."

"I wouldn't have let you, unless it was for me." The corners of his mouth twist up and he gives me an open smile. So cocky! I can't see his eyes, so I have no idea what's behind the smile. The pause is a second too long, and I feel a pang in my heart, as if wishing this wasn't just a joke. I can't let myself go on thinking like that. This is Miami, and people here are used to short-lived vacation romances. He's probably just another tourist looking for a good time. Then it hits me: so am I, in a way. I've never had a carefree, short-term relationship, but maybe that's exactly what I need right now—just some fun.

We're in the water, just floating around, letting the waves carry us up and down. It feels much warmer now, and I'm finally capable of catching my breath and talking.

"So, big guy, do you fall often?" I ask, smiling at the double meaning of the question.

"What do you think? Do I look like a guy who falls easily?"

"That would depend on a lot of things, things I don't know about you." I'm flirting and loving it.

"Like things you would like to learn about me?"

I take just a second too long before I reply, to enjoy the moment.

"Certainly not a bad idea." There, I let him know I'm interested, and it felt great.

"We could make that happen. Ask me something."

"Do you live here?"

"What do you think? Do I look like a local?"

"Let's see. You have a great tan, but that could work both ways, either living here or just vacationing. Then you have this British thing going, which could imply you're just visiting, although Miami is known to attract people from all over the world. I don't know."

"You've certainly done a good job observing me; this is kind of fun." He smiles and continues: "Let me guess, you're not a local, probably just vacationing." I nod and he continues.

"How long are you going to be here?" He looks at me through his shades, and I really want to see his eyes.

"I got too tired of everything and decided to take a few weeks to reenergize, three weeks actually. Just have some fun, you know?"

"You're lucky we met. I know the area pretty well, and we can make your stay a fun one. On second thought, I think we're both lucky."

I look at him and I can't take it anymore. I have to see his eyes. As the old saying goes, they *are* the mirrors to the soul...

"Do you always wear those shades? They're so dark, I bet you miss out on half the world." I try to make a joke out of it, since I feel awkward asking. He seems to read right through me.

"I can say the same about your polarized ones. I would love to see your eyes too. How about we keep the mystery going for a little longer, just for the kicks?"

I look at my reflection in his lenses and it dawns on me that we're both hidden by our shades, and bothered by it.

"Oh, so you like mystery huh? I can do mystery, Mr. Mystery Man."

He laughs hard and grabs my arms tight, pulling me deeper into the ocean. I know how to swim, but if I didn't, my life would be completely at his mercy. His touch feels so good that I don't let go, I just float next to him.

We turn in the water so I'm facing the shore. His face is lit up by the sun behind me and I can admire his masculine beauty. His hair is all wet and in disarray. Some of the locks fall to his forehead and eyes, and I can't help but touch them and brush them back. I feel my cheeks blushing again from the boldness of my actions. I barely recognize myself. I just went swimming while holding hands with a stranger, and now I'm touching him. Weird! This must be what the hot tropics do to people.

My thinking is interrupted when he grabs me by the waist and lifts me up, as he is jumping himself. His touch sends thrills down my body yet again, and I gasp and realize a strong wave just passed us.   He was making sure it wouldn't cover my head. The wave is gone, but his hands still linger at my waist.

"Are you cold? You're shivering." He runs his palms up and down my sides, touching my ribs just below the bikini top and going all the way down to my hips. The gesture is innocent, yet so sexy. My mouth opens in an 'o' to say something, but I'm frozen in the moment, just looking at him and imagining his hands touching me.

"Ok, there, dreamer, let's get you to dry land, then maybe we can catch some morning sun before it gets too hot." He lifts me and turns in the direction of the shore. Hugging me at the waist with one hand, he guides me out of the water, making sure the waves don't knock me off my feet.

I smile and follow him, as though it's the most natural thing. It amazes me how effortless it feels to be around him. Although, it's probably because we don't know each other. It's easy when it's just a casual encounter, two people looking for a little fun away from home. Is he away from home? He never really answered my question. I should ask again, but then again, should I? Does it even matter? I guess not.

"What are you thinking about? Your facial expression just went from dreamy to concerned and then back, all in a matter of seconds. I know women think a mile a minute but that was just too much. Did you realize you forgot something? Someone?" He looks at me with an amused smile.

I grin at his clever attempt to find out if he's got any competition around here. Got to give him credit, that was a rather creative way to ask. I wonder if he really did see all that on my face. I'm not used to people actually being interested in my emotions, let alone reading them.

"Nope, didn't forget anyone, not around here or anywhere else for that matter; and I know where my stuff is, assuming it's still there. Weren't you saying something about catching some morning sun? My building is that way. They might even have the beach chairs available by now. This city sure likes to sleep. Nothing is alive in the morning; it's like a ghost town." I catch myself blabbering on and on. I feel too out of my element inviting a stranger for, what should I even call it? We're outside, so I guess it's ok, right?

"Great, lead the way." I heard that last time, when we walked together to the parking lot. Although it doesn't seem Alex needs directions, neither now nor back then. We walk side by side, our hands brushing on occasion. I love every minute of it. I don't know what to say, but the silence isn't uncomfortable.

"Is this your first time in Miami?" He asks, looking straight ahead.

"No, I've been here a few times before."

"So, you know the area then?"

"I guess, but not that well. I usually stay around here."

"What's your favorite place?"

"Hard to say, probably the beach." I laugh, because that sounds silly.

"How about at night?" He asks with a smirk, and I spot the half-smile on his face again.

"I still like to be by the water, South Beach is pretty cool, a little too loud though." I turn my face to watch his reaction as I continue. "What's yours?"

"The beach is great. I know just the place on South Beach right by the ocean that is pretty quiet and serves great food and drinks." He's looking straight at me now.

"Would you like to go down there tonight?" He asks me so casually, as though he does it all the time. Maybe he does. What if he does? So what? I don't let myself wander to those thoughts. Betrayal is a feeling I know too intimately. Betrayal? Did I really just think that? Where did it even come from? This guy does not owe me a thing. I bite my lip and try to push these thoughts away.

"There, you're doing it again." He stops and turns to me, putting his thumb on my bottom lip to release it. I look up at his eyes, then lower, to his lips, wondering what a kiss would feel like. Oh god, is that me thinking? I don't recognize myself. Must be the sun around here..."

"Your face just went from happy to almost tortured, and now you're dreamy." I look up in his face and wonder how a stranger could read me so well.

"What's going on in that beautiful head of yours? Relax, you're on vacation, right? Enjoy it!"

His comments are right on the mark, and his observations are unbelievably accurate. Mind-reading capabilities—unbelievable. I'm on vacation. Isn't this what I just told myself? I'm blushing, so I look down and become really interested in the shells scattered across the sand. I look up at him once and smile sheepishly. "I must have really needed the vacation after all. Things have been pretty rough lately."

Suddenly my skin feels all too hot, either from the sun, or maybe it's from him. I know I just need to move forward before I spill too much of my personal stuff. As it is, he reads me all too well.
We're walking side by side again and no one says anything; it's as though he senses I need the

silence. Soon my bag is in sight, sitting on top of a chair with an umbrella. I point to it.

"Here, that's me. I'm going to ask for another chair." I walk up to the beach service booth and see Adrian there.

"Hi Adrian, could you get me one more chair for my friend?"

"For you, anything!" He smiles and walks out of the booth to the stack of chairs. When I turn around Alex is on the phone, looking irritated. I wonder where he got the phone from—I don't remember stopping anywhere near his things. That's strange at best. My thoughts are interrupted by Adrian.

"Did you run today? I didn't see you come out."

"I came out right after seven. Perfect time for a run, not too hot."

"I start at eight. I saw your things and decided to set you up."

"Thanks! Very thoughtful of you."

"No biggie, I said I'd take care of you." Adrian drags the chair across to the front row by the water, next to mine.

Chapter 7

Once everything is settled, I grab my bag and plop down. I need some sunblock pronto. I'm lucky if I haven't burned yet. I start rubbing it on over my legs, from ankles to the knees, to my thighs, working the lotion in circles. I raise my leg straight up to get to the back of my thigh and then I feel it. Alex's eyes are burning holes in my body. I feel on fire again. I tighten my stomach, instinctively lowering my leg and crossing it over the other. I clench my muscles and try to rid myself of the sexual tension that is building inside me again. He can't do this to me. Why am I feeling this way? Like a horny teenager.

Alex walks up to me slowly and says, without any question in his voice,

"Let me help you with that." His voice exudes confidence, and I hand him the lotion without a second thought. He squeezes a generous amount into his palm.

"Turn around." I do, completely hypnotized.

He rubs the lotion between his hands and touches my shoulders. I shiver and feel goosebumps all over my skin. He chuckles and starts working the lotion into my skin. His hands feel strong, yet gentle. He massages my shoulders, and I feel the muscles relaxing. He spreads the lotion over my upper back, then goes lower. I feel his hands on my lower back, thumbs gliding along my spine. I try to keep still and not show him the effect he's having on me. Then I feel his hands moving to my waist and up my ribs, passing my most ticklish point at the bottom rib. He stops just under my breasts and I take a sharp inhale. I feel his breath on my neck as he whispers into my ear, "Relax."

His voice is raspy. I turn my head around to see him and end up with my lips almost touching his.

"Thank you." I say it quietly, as if for his ears only.

"Do you need help with your back? I can return the favor..." I really want to touch him now, run my hands up and down his wide shoulders, exploring every curve of his muscles.

"I think I'm ok. Maybe later I will call on that favor." This sounds more like a promise, and I want to dare him to do it.

"You still need to finish your arms. Need help there?"

Yes, I want his hands on me again, touching and massaging me, but I have to control myself. So instead I say, "I think I can handle it."

I try to finish applying lotion as quickly as possible without getting distracted by him ogling me. All of a sudden, I feel super self-conscious touching myself in front of him, although rather innocently. It still feels seductive. Finally, I'm relieved to be done. I lie on my stomach and make a pillow out of my palms. I'm wearing only my swimming suit, so lying on my chest makes me feel more covered.

Alex is on his side, facing me, elbow propped under his head. His arm muscles are rippling. I use the benefit of the sunglasses covering my eyes and take time exploring his body. If I can't see his eyes, he shouldn't be able to see mine. I look lower at his chest. There is a light dusting of dark hair in the middle. His pectorals are perfectly defined. Looking lower, I see a thin trail of hair under his belly button that disappears into his trunks, right along the V of his muscles. Even when he's lying down, I can see the trunks are sitting low and seductively on his hips. I look lower, to his sculpted legs, with well-defined muscles. He reminds me of a Greek god, with this chiseled body and a perfect face. I look back up at his face and can't help but wonder what his eyes are like. I bet one look and I'll be gone.

He's looking back at me. I'm pretty sure he's studying every curve of my body while letting me study his. It should feel beyond awkward, but somehow it doesn't. I want him to know me better, to like me even. His self-confidence doesn't intimidate me, it excites me.

After what seems like long a time, he is the first one to break the silence.

"Tell me something about yourself." His head is no longer tilted downward, as though to let me know he's looking at my face and eyes, rather than being distracted by my body. I lift my face and look straight at him.

"I live in Chicago. It's cold and windy there now, so I'm super relieved to be here. How about you? Do you live here, or is this a vacation?" I want to know who he is, so I use the chance to ask questions. Normally, I'm rather reserved and don't like to pry.

"You could say both. I spend a lot of time here and run a business, but it feels too much like a vacation."

"I hear a hint of British accent and something else? Where are you from?"

"It's a long story, but I did study in London. What do you do?"

"I'm in the real estate business, working for a family company. What do you do around here?"

"I own a luxury boat rental company. Mixing business with pleasure. Boating is my biggest hobby."

"Must be amazing to do what you love. I think some call that the ultimate happiness, getting paid for your passion. I'm jealous."

"Don't be, it's just a matter of personal choice. The trick is that some make that choice and some don't."

I'm quiet now, thinking about what he said. It's so simple, yet so *not*. I wish I could make the choice. I wish I... I'm awakened from my thoughts by his thumb traveling across my forehead, gently smoothing out something there.

"When your mind wanders somewhere far away, you get this intense look on your face and a small vein on your forehead pops out and pulses."

I look at his face. I want to rip off those shades and finally see the eyes of the man who reads me like an open book.

"At least pretend there's some mystery left in me. Every woman has to feel mysterious, you know?" I try to distract him from this thought. Somehow, within just hours of knowing me, he has gotten dangerously close to my true feelings.

"Oh, there is plenty of mystery in you. I have no idea why you react to my words this way. I never know if the next thing I say will put you back in that place. It's like you're here one moment, then you're gone the next."

"Oh, I'm here, trust me. I'm just a little tired after running and swimming. The sun isn't helping either."

"Just take a nap, it's the best!" As he says it, he turns to his back and relaxes his shoulders.

"Great idea, are you going to do the same?" Smiling, I look over his delicious body, which he seems to be completely oblivious about.

"Yep, you bet I am!"

I grab my sun hat from my purse and cover my head, putting my cheek on my arm. I sneak one last look, and see his chest rising and falling as he takes deep breaths of air. Could he be anxious about something? He seems so confident, it hardly looks like a facade. Guys like him can have any girl they want. Oh, I'm not going to think like that; I know where that goes, and it's not pretty. I try to think of something nice instead, and my thoughts go back to the way Alex held my hand, held my body in the water, touched my back. I feel desire starting to build in my core. I want to feel his lips on mine, to know if he's a soft kisser, or passionate, or rough. I want to experience his touch, to feel his strong hands on me again. I want to be able to touch him, learn every inch of him. I drift to sleep and dream of him, his body against mine, his lips kissing my neck, behind my ear, then lower to my collar bone. He is kissing my shoulder, moving to the middle of my back, lingering there, going up to my neck. I feel feather kisses all over my back, and it sends shivers down my spine. I feel tingling between my legs, moisture building as my desire grows stronger. My breathing becomes more labored and I moan into his touch. I hear him whispering into my ear,
"You are so beautiful and sensual, even in your sleep."

Then something snaps inside of me and I realize I'm hearing his voice and feeling his touch, this is not just a dream. I jerk up, bump into his steel frame, and nearly fall off the chaise. His strong arms catch me and pull me into a hug. My heart is ready to jump out.

"Easy there, sleeping beauty, I didn't mean to scare you. You were sleeping, and your back was getting pink from the sun, so I just wanted to add some sunblock to cover it. Then you made these super sexy noises, and I couldn't help but whisper in your ear.

"Were you having a wet dream? Was I in it?" He's smiling widely at me, and I feel completely exposed in front of him. My nipples are poking out of my bikini, and I think my bottoms are soaking wet. I have to do something quick, before I blush and he reads right through me.

"Care for a swim?" As I'm asking him, I'm jumping off the chaise lounge and running toward the water. I dive in and gasp from contact with the cold waves. It's even worse than last time. The air leaves my lungs, and my body stiffens. I can't move from the shock. A big wave hits me and I'm upside down in the water, fighting my way back to my feet. Then, I feel a pair of strong arms grasping me and lifting my body up. As the last time, I find myself crushed against Alex's strong chest, his arms hugging me tightly. This time, I put my arms over his shoulders and around his neck.

"We're developing a certain trend here. Do you need CPR? I would be happy to administer it."

I look at him: face covered with beads of water, hair all wet and messy, lips slightly parted. I lean in and kiss him before I have time to think this through and change my mind. At first, it's just our lips nibbling each other, then I open my mouth slightly, and he takes it as an invitation to explore me further. Our tongues meet and dance together, teeth grazing, lips crushing.

I let my fingers run through his hair, pulling it slightly. His arms are traveling lower, to my waist and then to my hips. He pushes our bodies together and I feel his hard erection against my stomach. I grind against it and slide down his body, feeling him draw in a sharp breath. His fingers dig into my hips as he pushes my body against his in an effort to slow me down. I'm completely helpless in his arms, yet I feel more powerful than I ever did with a man before. I kiss him harder, fearing if I stop it will never be the same again. I want this moment to last. I'm not ready to let him go. How would I even look into his eyes after initiating this kiss attack? His eyes, I've never even seen them. God, what am I doing? I have to stop! This can't be right!

I break away from his lips, feeling completely breathless.

"I'm sorry! I don't know what happened! Sorry!"

I try to get free from his embrace and scramble out of water as fast as I can. I grab my beach bag on the way and run up the stairs to the hotel. I'm by the elevator in seconds, pushing the button to go up. It takes a few minutes for it to arrive, then the doors slowly open and I jump in and push the button for my floor. The doors start closing but then reopen again. I bate my breath and pray it's not him. I don't know what to say. I feel like a complete idiot. Running away to the water, then assaulting him with a kiss, only to run again. I'm standing soaking wet and dripping in the middle of the cool, air-conditioned space, shaking cold. Then I see him, entering the elevator. I look down and do not dare to look back up. As the elevator doors close, he comes near me and puts his forefinger under my chin, lifting it. I look up at him and see his face inches from me, his ragged breath mixes with mine. I have no words.

He lowers his lips and kisses me again. Putting his fingers in my wet hair and running his other hand down to the small of my back.

This kiss is so much softer and gentler, as though he is afraid to scare me off again.

Then he breaks it and says, "It's ok. Don't panic. And please don't run from me again. You know I'll catch you." He places another kiss as the elevator doors open.

I don't know what to do. Do we go back down, or do we go inside?

He takes my hand and leads me out to the floor. "You're shaking cold, you need a hot shower before you end up stuck in bed for most of your vacation."

I find my voice and ask, "Would you like to come in?

You must be cold yourself."

"I would love to, as long as you're ok with it. I just didn't want to let you run away from me like that. I'm attracted to you, and I'd say it's safe to assume the feeling is mutual." Holding my shaking hands in his, he runs slow circles with his thumbs, calming me. His voice is quieter now.

"I think it's great, but I see you're fighting it, and I don't know why. So unless you're really ok, I would rather not push you." He's silent now, waiting for my response, still gently holding my hands.

I look at him and feel utterly stupid for acting like a schoolgirl. So I smile and say, "Hey, I need you to do me a favor."

His eyebrows shoot up over his shades from the surprise. "That's the last thing I expected you to say. You never cease to surprise me. What would that it be?" One corner of his mouth lifts up in a trademark smile I'm really starting to like.

I take a second too long to answer, making sure his anticipation builds.

"Take off your sunglasses. I'm dying to see your eyes."

He nods and smiles, seeming to like my idea.

"How about we do it together?"

He steps closer to me and puts his hands on my cheeks, fingers touching my shades. I nod and raise my palms to his face. We lift each other's sunglasses away and lock eyes for the first time. I get lost in his sparkling deep blues, drowning in their depth. The color looks almost electric bright. I see him gazing into my honey-hazel ones and beaming with a full smile.

"You are very beautiful, you know that?"

I try not to shy away. "You're not so bad yourself."

He plants a quick peck on my lips. "Let's get you warmed up before you catch pneumonia and I'm forced to stay by your bed. I'd rather have other pretenses for that."

Now he's openly laughing at me, and I blush at the mention of him and my bed.

I quickly turn and lead the way to my condo. He grabs me by the arm and turns in place. "Don't run! It won't help you or save you. Just let it go, stop fighting yourself." I look up into his eyes and genuinely promise, "I'll try."
He hugs me and presses me hard against his body. I feel his cold skin against my cheek and realize we're still in the hallway, cold and shivering, right in front of my door. "We're here, this is me."

He lets go of his hold just slightly so I can get my hand into the bag and dig out the key card. Once I put it in and push the door open, he lifts me into his arms and carries me inside, pushing the door closed with his foot. He follows through the living area and to the bedroom suite, locating the bathroom door rather quickly. We're in the shower cabin in seconds, with the water splashing at us. It's cold, and I stifle a scream as it runs down my back. Grabbing onto his body harder to find shelter from the cold water, I feel him holding me tight. In seconds the water warms up, and soon it's hot and steamy. He puts me down on my feet for a moment before lifting and pushing me against the shower wall. My back comes in contact with cold tiles and I grab onto him in an effort to minimize my exposure to the icy-cold granite surface. My arms are on his shoulders, back arching, chest rising up. Instantly his lips are on mine, devouring me. Sneaking his arms under my butt, lifting me higher, he levels my shoulders with his face. I'm so high I can no longer reach his lips. I sigh at the loss, only to gasp at the feel of his mouth on my neck, right under my chin. His stubble grazes my skin, and I push a little against his mouth. I want no space between us, I want to feel him on me, over me, in me. He makes a trail of wet kisses down my neck and to the swell of my breasts. He looks up at me for a second, as if asking if I'm ok with him kissing me there, and I nod and close my eyes. That's all the approval he needs, and I feel his lips in the space between my breasts. I arch my back instinctively, effectively pushing my chest into his face. I try to wiggle away, but he holds me tighter, moving one arm up to bring me closer to his lips.

"Let go." He starts kissing my breasts, while pulling on the string holding the bikini top in place.

"May I?" That's all he says, asking to untie my top and bare the rest of my breasts. I nod and try to hold on to him tighter to hide my nakedness. His fingers make quick work of the clasp, and I feel my bikini top loosening up.

The bra triangles, heavy with water, stay in place, as if glued to my skin. He grabs the edge of one of them with his teeth and drags away. My taut nipple pops out and he sucks on it, biting ever so lightly. It sends a tide of pleasure through my whole body, culminating in my core. I start breathing heavily and after a few seconds, I grind my pelvis against him. I need to feel some pressure there. I'm so slick from my arousal that the bikini slides up and down as I grind against his steel abs. He groans and runs his hand down my back and to my hip, slowly nearing my hot spot. I push against him again, as if inviting him. He no longer hesitates. His fingers push away the wet fabric of my swimming suit and touch me. I inhale sharply and without thinking, push into him again. His finger makes it inside of me, and he starts rubbing a sweet spot I didn't know existed. I gasp and push into him harder, wanting more. He slides another finger in while running circles around my clit with his thumb.

All the while his mouth is on my nipple, kissing, sucking, licking. I'm overwhelmed by the sensations, unable to contain myself any longer. Carnal sounds are escaping my mouth. I'm moaning and writhing in his arms. I feel myself getting closer, the coils getting tighter, and I try to squeeze my legs to make it last longer. I'm losing this battle, but I try to stay in control.

"Let go." I hear his raspy voice, and it's my undoing. I come so hard I scream his name. I'm shuddering and riding out the waves of an incredible orgasm. Wave after wave, it cascades through my body, leaving me boneless. I peel my eyes open and see Alex looking at me, smiling. He kisses my lips gently, first taking my lower lip in his mouth, grazing it with his teeth and licking it with his tongue before moving on to my upper lip, repeating the same thing. I close my eyes again, getting lost in him.

Finally, I look at him and smile. "This was amazing, I ... I ..." He puts his lips on mine again and does not let me finish.

"You don't have to say anything. I'm happy you enjoyed it. I hope to give you many more." He has a wicked smile on his face now. I'm lowered to the floor, and I realize my legs are shaking. I keep a strong hold on his shoulders and lean in closer.

"I hope so too," I whisper as I tuck my face into the crook of his neck. His thumb finds my chin, lifting my face up.

"Please stop shying away. There's nothing wrong with what we're doing."
I nod and lower my eyelashes. He plants a soft kiss on my forehead, and it feels more intimate than anything we've done so far. Then he takes a sponge, squirts some body wash on it, and starts running it along my shoulders and arms, making his way to my chest. It's still partially hidden away by the wet triangles of the bikini top. He works the

sponge around and soon my breasts are covered in white foam, the bra long gone. I cross my arms over my chest, pushing cleavage up, but at least covering the nipples. He genuinely laughs at me.

"You are hopeless, I just kissed you there bare naked and you were ok, but now you're suddenly self-conscious? I don't get it."

"I know you probably hear this all the time, but I'm really never like this. I mean, never."

Alex stops washing my naked body and steps closer to me, placing both hands on the wall and encasing me in his space. His face is serious, eyes trained on mine.

He looks at me long and hard. "I was just teasing you. I know this isn't who you are, and I realize this isn't your thing. And contrary to what you're assuming, I *don't* hear things like that all the time. Believe it or not, I'm pretty reserved when it comes to women. I am not a monk by any means, but random hookups aren't my thing either. And this is special." He looks sincere. Maybe even too serious.

I am so confused I don't know what to say. He's nothing like I thought he'd be. This was supposed to be an easy, vacation fling. Now I don't know what to believe, so I just leave it alone for now and shyly smile back at him. "It *is* special."

The expression on his face is unreadable, and before I have another look, he turns me around and runs a sponge over my back and hips, lowering to wash my legs. We're both still wearing our bottoms, and it doesn't feel right to remove them now. As if sensing my discomfort, he doesn't say anything else, and washes himself after he's done with me. I feel the air thick with awkwardness, and I try to lighten things up.

"You're going to smell like a girl." I steal a look at his practically naked body sans swimming trunks. He is handsome to perfection, lean and built, yet not too bulky. I finish studying his perfect planes and our eyes meet. Pink crawls into my cheeks and as always, Alex notices. I maintain eye contact, despite desperately wanting to break it and shy away.

Alex's voice comes out raspy and sexy: "I don't think you should complain about that." His lopsided smile says he's enjoying the moment, awkwardness forgotten.

"No complaints!" I smile, realizing what he's implying. He smells like a girl, like me. This is my claim on him, if only temporary. Temporary—this is the reality. Wasn't that what I wanted to begin with? I guess old habits die hard. I'm a relationship kind of girl. I know I have no right to demand anything from him. I knew what I was getting myself into from the beginning. Why is it, then, that I think back to what he said, about this being special? I'm just hopeless at this vacation-fling stuff.

"Would you stop?!" He's in my face, hands on my shoulders, breathing hard, eyes on fire. I jerk at his loud voice and the feel of strong hands on my delicate shoulders. I'm so small next to him, it's scary. My mouth falls open. What is he talking about?

"You're far away again, and it's not a good place. There's pain on your face. What did I say? Why do I keep losing you like this?" His breathing is heavy, and his eyes are piercing right through me, into my soul. I'm afraid to break under the intensity of his stare. Blinking a few times at him, I feel tingling in my eyes, and I pray inwardly that I can stay strong and keep from crying. I don't know what to say. I feel so badly for him. He must think it's his fault somehow. Still, I'm not ready to talk about my life. I really like this girl I'm pretending to be: young, happy, carefree. I'm not ready to unload the burden of my past onto him and risk scaring him away.

"I don't know... it's not you... just something on my mind. I don't want to talk about it." I'm blabbering, trying to get through the moment as quickly as I can.

He gently wraps his arms around me and rubs circles along my back, then moves up to my nape and threads his fingers through my tangled curls. I melt into his hug and inhale the smell of his skin mixed with my soap. It's perfect!

"Ok, let's get out of here." He lifts me up again, as if I weigh nothing, and steps onto the mat outside the shower. I keep my arms at my chest, and Alex wraps a plush towel around my shoulders. My arms squeeze out one by one and make a quick work of wrapping my body tightly and securing the end of the towel. Alex uses the second towel, his movements leisurely, but efficient. He exudes undeniable confidence.

"You know, we could remove our wet bottoms, throw them in the dryer, wrap ourselves in these huge towels and just relax." I'm offering bold things again, and try to keep looking at him without lowering my gaze to the floor. He lifts an eyebrow, his lips stretching in such a familiar smile that I just can't take it. His eyes are seeing right into me, into the space inside my soul that's full of insecurities, sadness, and betrayal. I break the stare and look down.

"You almost kept looking at me without casting your eyes away. We should reward you for it." He removes his trunks under the towel. "Where is the dryer?"

I take mine off and gather all the wet pieces together. We step out of the steamy bathroom into the crisp, air-conditioned room. I make a beeline to the dryer, throw everything in, and power it on. I turn around and bump right into a strong and familiar chest. Alex is towering over me, a playful spark in his eyes.

"Come here before you freeze." He lifts me up again, and I giggle as his fingers touch my ticklish spot.

"Are you ticklish?" The playful sparks in his eyes light up even more, and I know I'm in trouble now.

Trying to play it cool, I ask nonchalantly, "No, why would you think that?"

Chapter 8

His smile is full on, and little sparks dance in his blue eyes.

"I don't know, maybe because you giggled when I touched you here."

He runs his fingers along my ribs, looking for that one spot, and soon he's rewarded with another round of my uncontrollable giggles. We are a messy tangle of arms and legs. I'm not sure when or how, but we end up on my bed, him hovering over me, keeping his weight on his elbows while effectively trapping me underneath. I try to catch my breath, look in his eyes, and get lost in those blues all over again. It seems they're a shade darker now, indigo blue, filled with desire. He lowers his mouth to mine and we kiss, passionately, not able to get enough of each other. I run my hands to the back of his neck and through his hair. The locks feel wet and silky between my fingers. I pull him closer, wanting more. His chest is against mine, and I feel some of his weight on me. I love it. I'm out of breath and feeling dizzy, lips swollen, eyes rolling back. He slows the kiss, watching my reaction. I open my eyes, feeling his gaze hot on my face.

"Look at me."

He commands before I have a chance to look away. My eyes are instantly on his. He lowers his mouth on mine and gives me another slow, gentle kiss, stopping only to make a trail of feather-light kisses along my jaw line and down to my neck. My pulse is beating so fast and loud it's deafening. He trails the kisses down my neck and finds my pulsing artery. His tongue is running along it, and I feel tingling desire spread through my body. Alex continues licking and sucking my neck and soon, I'm writhing under him, panting and clawing at the mattress.

He stops and raises his face to look at me. My cheeks are flushed and my hair is scattered around my face. It's drying into an unruly mass of curls and tangles. He smiles and looks at my hair, cheeks, neck, swollen lips, finally stopping at my desire-filled eyes.

"You are so beautiful. I want to make love to you until you're so uninhibited you scream out all your desires, staring me straight in the eyes, without being able to control yourself. I want you moaning my name over and over when you come."

A tight coil starts building somewhere deep inside of me. His words are so carnal. I don't know what one is supposed to say to that. We met just a few days ago, yet we're already in my bed, about to make love. Strangely enough, I feel completely safe in his arms. Am I making a mistake? Is this ok? I never would have done anything like this in Chicago. Is this what people do on vacations? These thoughts run through my mind like a whirlwind. Then I feel his soft kiss on my forehead.

Lifting his lips just barely away from me he is whispering, "Stop analyzing and worrying. Just live and enjoy. Give me a chance to show you."

I'm not even sure what he's talking about anymore. Is it sex? Is it life? Relationships? Friendship? It can't be that complicated; he doesn't know me at all. My mind screams stop and get out before it's too late, but my traitorous body wants him with me, on me, in me. My mind loses the battle, and I take his face with both my hands and start kissing him like my life depends on it, as if he really could solve all my problems and teach me to live my life to the fullest.

His lips are instantly on mine, devouring my mouth, exploring every detail, taking everything I have to offer. He leans on his side and frees one arm to roam my body, starting with my neckline and shoulders and moving lower to undo my towel. Once I'm no longer covered, he breaks the kiss to look at me, and I feel crimson creeping up my cheeks. He runs his palm down my chest to cup my breast. His forefinger is drawing circles on my flesh and my nipples pucker up. He takes one between his fingers and rolls it lightly, then a little stronger. A moan escapes my mouth, and I try to catch my breath. He seems to play my body like a musical instrument, perfectly in tune, the slightest touch making my nerves sing.

Lowering his head, he takes my other nipple in his mouth and sucks it gently at first, then bites down lightly and grazes it with his teeth. Now the pleasure shoots through me like an electric shock. I moan and pant and try to grind my hips against him. As if on cue, he follows a trail of light touches down my body and soon his hand is on my hip, going to the crease between my legs. I instinctively tighten my muscles and push my legs together. His touch is gentle yet determined.

"Let go."

He whispers softly, pushing away my inhibitions. My muscles relax on their own accord. His hand follows down my folds and connects with my soaking wet core. He takes a sharp breath in and out.

"You are so wet; I didn't realize you were so aroused for me."

His fingers spread the moisture around, drawing slow circles around my sex. As the circles get smaller and smaller his fingers find their way into my body. I gasp as he pushes a digit inside of me.

"You are so tight, so perfect!"

His finger starts moving in me, slow and tentative. Then he adds another one and I gasp again at being stretched further. His thumb finds my sensitive nub and touches it lightly. A shockwave shoots through me, and I lift my hips to meet his hand.

"Shhh, easy, easy."

He touches my clit, this time pushing a little harder and not breaking contact. I scream and jerk my hips. I want him desperately. He pulls his fingers slightly out and as I lift my hips, he slams his hand down to meet me. His mouth is on my breast, licking, twisting, biting. I start shaking as he continues pulling his fingers out slowly and plunging them in sharply, all the while rubbing my clit with his thumb. I scream and lose myself in ecstasy.

"Yes ... yes ... don't stop, Alex, oh, oh ..."

I scream as I come and tighten around his fingers. As soon as the last words fly off my lips, his mouth is on mine, kissing me roughly. He can't control himself. I can sense he's on the brink.

"I want you. Inside of me. Now."

It's a plea more than a command, but he obliges instantly. Alex unwraps his towel and hovers over me, but doesn't try to make contact.
Pulling away from my lips he asks.

"Condoms?"

"I've got none, I'm on birth control. You?"

"I've got none on me either. I'm clean. I never, god this sounds bad, I never do this with anyone without protection. You don't have to believe me. We don't have to do this."

His voice is desperate. He starts to pull away, but I don't let him.

"I trust you. Maybe I shouldn't, but I do." Our eyes meet and say more than the words can. There is mutual trust and understanding. I see we both are affected by this.

"Your trust means a lot to me."

He lowers his mouth on mine and I lift my hips to meet his. He guides himself to my entrance and pushes in slightly. I tense at the feeling of his width.

"Relax, I won't hurt you. We'll take it slowly. You're so tight, it's incredible."

I try to relax and he pulls out a little, only to push in more. I tense and he pulls out. His fingers find my clit and start rubbing slow, gentle circles. I relax and feel warmth coursing through my body. He enters me again, very slowly, this time a little deeper, then stops. Instead of pulling out, he angles his body and moves inside of me. This change in angle puts his cock right at my sensitive spot, and I whimper with pleasure. He pushes in a little more until he is completely buried in me. I feel I'm being stretched to the limit, but it's pleasant. Still rubbing my clit, he starts moving in and out, slowly at first, but increasing speed with each thrust. I lift my hips to meet his thrusts. Then, in one swift motion, he hugs me and lifts my butt while turning us around. I'm straddling him now.   My palms rest against his chest and I start moving, rubbing myself against him. We're feeling each other, learning our bodies, finding our rhythm. I'm overwhelmed by the sudden power exchange. He went from taking charge, to completely submitting to my lead. This is very unfamiliar to me. I learn to move and set the pace, as if this is my first time.

His hands let go of my waist and start gliding along my body, from hips to the waist line and up to the underside of my breasts. Sunlight filters in through the sheer curtains, and I feel overly exposed, but I use all the willpower I can summon to keep me from throwing my arms over my chest and hiding away.

His eyes are darker now, pupils dilated and drowning in desire. He looks at me, and I marvel at the effect I have on him. He cups my breasts and rolls both nipples between his fingers, pinching them. This sends a shot through my body and straight to my core. I scream and start riding him rougher, lifting up higher and plunging him into me deep. Now it's his turn to grasp for self-control. He groans loudly, lifts, and tries to hold my body still for a second. I bite my lip and look down. There he is, this absolutely stunning male who can barely contain himself and the best part is, I did it.
My palms run over my nipples and I tug them. He groans loudly and loosens his hold just a bit. Using the opportunity, I lift up and grind against him. This puts me closer to the edge, and I slow down. I don't want it to be over, not yet. I rotate my hips with him deep inside of me. I try a new, slow pace, just barely lifting up, and then gently lowering down. The orgasm is building and I can barely control it. I start trembling.

"Just let go, I want to hear you come. Come for me!"

I lift higher and plunge sharply down, throwing myself over the edge. I start shaking and he takes over, holding me up and moving his hips to meet my thighs. I'm shuddering, screaming his name over and over. When I can no longer hold up, he twists us around and I'm on the bottom again. He's over me, kissing my neck and whispering in my ear. He continues moving, letting me ride out the last wave of my orgasm. Before it fully passes, he lifts his torso and assaults me with a series of deep, strong thrusts. Spreading my legs wide, he plunges in and out of me over and over. I will my eyes to stay open and watch his face. The beauty of his raw emotion is indescribable. The pressure inside me is building with renewed force.

"I'm almost there, let's come together! Now!"

I start contracting around his cock. Another thrust and we're gone. He roars my name and slams into me time after time, filling me with his hot cum. I feel it spilling out. His pace slows down and we both breathe through the remnants of our orgasms. His breathing is ragged, then he crashes down on me, barely holding himself up on his elbows. He kisses me madly, devouring my mouth and sucking on my bottom lip. I pull him to me and run my nails along his back, wanting more contact. He pushes a little more into the mattress and I feel his weight on me. I love it.

We are still for minutes, catching our breath, with him still buried deep inside me. I don't want to let go. I feel safe and wanted here. I haven't felt this way in ages, if ever.

Slowly, he rolls to his back, taking me with him. Now I'm on top again, still fully connected. I don't intend to let go, not any time soon.

"You like me inside of you, don't you?"

I smile and cast my eyes downward, stealing a glimpse of how our bodies connect, fitting perfectly together.

"What makes you say that?"

"Look at me, stop shying away. I want you to be completely uninhibited with me. Say what you want, do what you want. I want to know all of you, everything that is hiding behind the sadness in your eyes. I can't get enough of you. I'm crazy about you! You are sexy as hell, and you should know it. I love being inside of you too. This feeling of no barriers, just us, it's unreal..."

I look at his eyes and wonder why I couldn't have met him earlier. My life could have been so different. He wants me, and doesn't care if I'm successful, or rich, or well-connected. None of that matters to him.

He pulls my face to his and kisses my forehead ever so gently.

"What's going on in that beautiful mind of yours? Will you ever tell me? It's almost like I'm seeing the tip of the iceberg, and what's under water is infinitely bigger, more beautiful, and more complex than what's on top. I want to know you, *all* of you."

His words run through my ears. This can't be true. Aren't I just a fling to him? Maybe it's been a little more romantic than your average fling, but still, it's just a *fling*, right? My head is swimming with questions and possible answers.

"It's ok, don't say anything. We'll take it slow, ok? I'm not going to push you."

He lowers my head to his chest and hugs me tight. I'm exhausted and relax into his arms. Soon, I'm drifting away, and the feel of his body under me and his arms around me is the most wonderful thing. The steady beat of his heart calms and grounds me.

Minutes go by, maybe even an hour. I'm brought back to the reality when he starts gently stirring around me. Wow, did we just fall asleep like this, together? I lift my head to find his smiling face looking at me.

"You are so peaceful in your sleep. I didn't mean to wake you, just couldn't resist touching you."

"Oh, how long has it been?"

"I don't know and I don't care."

"I guess I don't care either."

I smile and lower my lips to kiss him. Then I feel his erection waking up inside of me.

"Are we still? Uh..." I can't say it out loud.

"Yes, I'm still buried inside of you, and I love it!"

I try to hide my face in the crook of his neck, but he catches me before I have a chance.

"Look at me. Kiss me."

I follow and kiss him passionately, feeling his erection growing to its full length. I tighten my core muscles and he gasps.

"A little naughty, aren't you?"

I don't reply, just kiss him harder and shift on top of him. First slowly, grinding my clit against him, getting more aroused. Then I rise up and ride him, lifting up and plunging down. He matches my every thrust, lifting his hips to meet mine. Being on top, I enjoy a good view of him. Narrow hips with a well-defined V, chiseled pectorals, wide shoulders with sculpted muscles, and strong arms. His nipples are flat and taut when I run my fingers over them. He seems to enjoy the view he's getting himself. In the heat of the moment, I forgot yet again how exposed I am. His hands are on my hips, moving up to cup my breasts. He rolls my nipples and pulls on them to elongate them into sharp peaks. The sensations run though my body and I find it difficult to stay upward. The next moment, I'm on my side, one leg in the air. He is thrusting into me, going even deeper than before. This position lets him stimulate new areas, and I'm so close now. I wiggle out of his grip and turn my butt up to him.

"Naughty, naughty little girl."

He holds my hips and guides his cock back in, slowly at first, but gripping me hard at the last moment and thrusting roughly into me. I gasp and try to support myself on my elbows. He wraps his hand around me, pulling me up, and reaches to cup my breasts. I straighten up against his chest, and he goes for my clit with his other hand. We are doing a slow dance, so I take the lead and rub against him, up and down.

My body is pressed tight against his. His lips are on my neck, sucking and biting. I run my fingers into his curls, pushing him closer to me. His teeth grind against my skin and I tremble. He pushes me forward on the bed, spreads my legs wide and lies on top of me. His cocks finds a way back into my body and he works it against me. I have the feel of his steel frame on top of mine. The weight and strength are not scary or intimidating, instead I feel cherished and protected. I feel worshipped.

He kisses between my shoulders, sending thrills down to my toes. I never even suspected this was an erogenous zone for me. I turn my head and try to look up at him. His face is tense, like he's afraid to let go too soon.

"I'm almost there."

I slide my hand under my belly to touch my clit and feel his fingers lacing with mine and rubbing against me. Then he turns me over and I'm still on the bottom, with him between my legs. His fingers are on my clit, I cover them with mine and guide his moves. He plunges into me and moves in a perfect rhythm, our own rhythm. It's amazing how we feel each other, knowing just how to move.

"Let's do it together again."

I'm looking him straight in the eyes as I say it, and realize I'm comfortable, not shying away as usual.

"Oh yeah, baby! Together! Now!" His fingers run a full circle around my clit culminating at the center with a bit more pressure while his hips push hard into me. His words combined with skills and an intuitive knowledge of my body are my downfall. I come apart in front of him, putting every ounce of my remaining energy into an effort to keep my eyes open. Our eyes are locked as he lowers to kiss me. I let go entirely and my muscles contract around his length, sending him over the edge. His eyes are trained on me, and I realize he is struggling to keep them open. I look straight into the deep blues as we both come apart. The feeling is unreal, as if looking into someone's bared sole, no disguises, no pretenses.

A single tear runs down my cheek and I try to wipe it before he realizes it was there. As always, nothing escapes his attention. He lowers down, cradling himself between my legs, his face inches from mine. Our stomachs and chests are touching, leaving no space in between. His face is full of concern. The lighthearted expression that's usually there is gone, replaced by a pain that's hard to describe.

"Did I hurt you? Tell me. I'm sorry, I never meant to cause you any pain."

This is such a different Alex, a side of him I've never seen, something so vulnerable, hidden so deep it never surfaces.

"No, you did not hurt me. It's not that. I just....it was so beautiful and intense. I never looked someone in the eyes like that."

A sigh of relief escapes his lips and the painful expression slowly fades away, replaced by his usual, calm look.

"I thought I hurt you. I saw the tear and I didn't know what to think."

While his face looks calm, his voice betrays him and comes out a bit shaky.

"Why did you suddenly get worried, almost panicky? The pain on your face looked unbearable."

A shadow crosses over his features, and is gone in seconds.

"Perhaps someday, not now. We both have our life stories to tell, let's not do it now."

I can relate to that, so I don't push it. I would hate if he did that to me.

"Let's take a shower before we fall asleep again." I smile at him and wink.

"We can actually do it without our clothes this time." I'm giggling now to hide my self-consciousness, and he sees right through it.

"You're beautiful. Embrace it!" He lifts himself off me and pulls his length out. We fit so perfectly together, and I wince at the loss. He smiles knowingly.

"Kind of got used it already, huh?" I flush crimson, and he extends his arms and pulls me up to him.

"You are something else; I have never met anyone like you."

"Why?"

"I guess luck was not on my side."

"Same here I guess."

"I would hope so."

He lifts me into his arms and carries me back to the shower. This time he lets the water run down first and steps in after it's warm. I slide down his bare chest and stand on the shower tiles.

"I want to wash you."

I feel the need to show him how much I care. I think washing each other is a deeply intimate act. I take a sponge and add a generous amount of shower gel. It glides around his shoulders, then lower, to the dusting of hair on his chest. My other hand touches and explores his body, as if trying to memorize every curve, every ridge. He is still under my touch, except for his fingers playing with my wet curls. I take my time and go over every inch of his chest and shoulders, drawing slow, teasing circles.

"You are so beautiful," he says, as his lips find mine. He sucks on my lower lip gently, then teases it with his tongue. He breaks the kiss, turns me in place so my back is to him, and starts working the sponge from my neck down my back and around my waist to my breasts.

I give up the sponge along with my perceived control. How is it possible I feel powerful one minute and completely at his mercy the next? This emotional roller-coaster is unfamiliar to me. It's exciting and exhausting at once. I seem to have had more emotions running through me in these past few days than in the past year. I have to keep my head straight, or I'll be a wreck when this is over. This is too good. Like all fairytales, this one won't last forever. It would have to be over, it's just a fling, a vacation romance sparked by the sun and the heat. I will, however, enjoy it while I can. I just hope to god it doesn't consume and crash me in the process.

Maybe we should take it slower. I can't think with his hands and lips on me. So that's it, one more time, and then we slow down. I make a deal with my traitorous body and turn around to find his lips. I take his mouth in mine and dig my hands in his hair. My leg wraps around hips while I rub my pelvis against his erection. He grabs my bottom with both hands and lifts me up. I wrap both legs around his waist and thrust against him. No words are needed, he knows exactly what I want and how. He guides his cock inside of me, slowly pushing in, and I marvel at the sensation of being filled to the brim. I tighten my core muscles, and he groans in response. Then we start our slow dance, my body meeting his, thrust for thrust, our bodies melting into one. The water pours down, washing away all the moisture created by our arousal, creating friction between us. A shudder runs through me with each new thrust, and I can't take it any longer. My over-sensitized body is on the brink of another explosion.

"Oh god, I'm so close, come with me, come with me!"

"Emmeline!"

It's not a word, it's a cry from somewhere deep inside of him. He thrusts into me several more times, and we both shatter to pieces, orgasms taking us. I grip him tight, pull his hair and bite down on his lip. His fingers dig into my thighs, and it's sure to leave bruises. We're marking each other as our own.

As we are coming down from the high I loosen my grip and let go of his lip only to find I bit him too hard. There's a drop of blood there. I panic. I can't believe I hurt him like that. How did I lose control? How did I not see I was doing this? I kiss his lips, licking the blood away, running my tongue over his lip to taste if there is more coming.

"I hurt you, I'm sorry, I'm so sorry. I don't know what happened, I didn't realize I was biting you. Is it bad?" My eyes are panicking and pleading with him. He nudges the tip of my nose with his and smiles.
"Stop! No worries, remember! Just kiss me."

"You aren't in pain?"

"No. Kiss me, now!" And so I oblige. I kiss him gently and run my tongue over his lip again and again, making sure there's no more blood.

"Ok, easy there now, unless you want round two before we leave the shower." He smiles down at me, and I realize he's still inside of me, and I can feel him growing. I can't believe this guy. Doesn't he need rest? At this pace, I won't be able to walk. As it is, I am pretty sore after the last time. Water with the lack of lubricant to blame.

"Wow, don't you need a break or something?" He just laughs and slides me off his length.

"You need a break, or else I'll be stuck carrying you around, since you'll lack the ability to walk. On second thought, this might be a great idea; you'll stop running away from me." He tries to slip back inside of me, and I smack him playfully to break free.

"Ok, how about we finish the shower and you get ready? I'll make a quick run to my place, change, and pick you up in half an hour. We can go for dinner, then maybe a walk. I'll show you a few cool places around South Beach."

"Sounds like a plan. Where are we going?"

"It'll be a surprise. Do you have any preferences?"

"I have one request." I'm met with his lopsided smile and a raised brow.

"We're taking my car. I rented a convertible, and I intend on enjoying it while I'm here. I'll drive, and you'll tell me where to go."

I stare him straight in the eyes with a determined look and a mischievous smile.

"How come you didn't ask if I have a fun car? What if I have a convertible too?" He practically pouts before breaking into a laugh.

"It doesn't matter. You can ride in a new car—should be fun—and I get to drive my Audi. Besides, I would never drive a car that isn't mine. So, are you in?"

Alex actually rolls his eyes at me, knowing full well he doesn't have a choice in the matter.

"You are something else. Usually women try to lure men out to their cars, just to see the ride and assess the male. You almost hurt my feelings by being so openly disinterested." I just shrug.

"Really, I think it's just boys and their toys. You guys are obsessed with them and think we actually care."

"I love my car, but that's not the point."

"Proves my point exactly." I laugh at him and he smiles back. There is something in that smile that is deeper than the simple joke. I can't place it, and the look is gone before I get to examine it more closely.

"So, I will see you in the lobby in half an hour. Will that be enough time for you to get ready? Or do you need an hour?"

"Half an hour should be good, and if I'm late, don't take it personally. I'm going to take some time getting control of my crazy curls."

"No, leave them alone, and down, just like now. You look magical. Don't even waste your time."

"This is not my look, I'm never this crazy and wild."

"I can tell. I see it, but nonetheless I love your hair raw and untamed. Maybe you should consider reinventing your style."

At some point, I feel we're no longer just talking about my hair. How does he know? How does he sense it? His thumb runs across my forehead, and I look into his eyes.

"You're doing it again. Stop. Just get ready and be yourself, no need to go through the trouble of perfecting something that's already perfect."

He places a gentle kiss on my forehead and steps out of the shower. Wrapping a towel around his waist, he walks out of the bathroom in search of his now-dry swimming trunks. The door closes behind him, and I'm left with my thoughts. Why couldn't I have met Alex under different circumstances, when we could have had a future together?

Chapter 9

I decide to follow Alex's advice and waste no time. After a quick towel drying, I head straight to the walk-in closet, where my clothes are hanging neatly. Being an obsessive control freak has its advantages. I flip through my outfits in search of something light, casual yet elegant. A perfect outfit is staring right at me. A white strapless dress that hugs my chest and waist in just the right way, with the skirt flowing down my hips to my knee. It's practically see-through, so I decide on nude underwear, to create a naked look. I love white. Whether it's linens or heavy sweaters, I'm a sucker for white. Too bad I don't get to wear it often. My business wardrobe is primarily navy blues and charcoal greys, highlighted by the occasional pastel. I'm going to take full advantage of being in Miami. In fact, I need to go shopping tomorrow and pick out a few more white outfits, preferably linen. They would be perfect in this humid, hot weather.

I finish my outfit with a pair of white platform sandals that tie around my ankles. The white looks perfect against my now-tanned skin, the platforms making me just a bit taller and giving my legs a few extra inches, the ankle ties accentuating the look. I grab a white scarf to go over my shoulders in case I get chilly in the air-conditioned restaurant, and also to cover my hair while driving.

Looking at myself in the mirror, I realize I like my hair curly and messy. Besides, I cannot win the battle against the humidity here, especially if we're going to be driving with the top down.

And the last step: makeup. I want nothing dark or heavy, instead opting for a light, shimmery look. I apply a silvery, powdered eye shadow that makes my already big eyes look even bigger. A layer of mascara, some lip gloss, a quick spritz of my favorite perfume, and I'm ready to go.

One last glance in the mirror reveals very few similarities with the girl who came here a few days ago. A tired look and sad eyes are replaced with flushed cheeks and a smile that lights up my whole face and finally touches my eyes. The curls make me look much younger than my 27 years, especially combined with my barely-there makeup. The change is striking.

As I put on my white-gold watch, a graduation present from my parents, I realize the timing is perfect. I'm not late, even a few minutes early. The valet guy takes my ticket and is on his way to get the car. I'm waiting patiently until I see it pulling up from around the corner. I step forward and get in as soon as the valet gets out. I put the top down and wait for Alex. Checking the instrument panel for GPS, I fail to notice him standing by the car. At some point I feel eyes on me, and I know it's him even before I turn my head. I finally turn around to see a gorgeous male standing right by my car door, just a step behind me. He looks even better than he did on the beach, if that's possible. He is wearing a white shirt with the top few buttons open, sleeves rolled up to reveal a pair of strong arms. The shirt hugs his muscular chest and hangs loosely around his waist. A pair of washed, light blue denims hangs low on his hips. I am openly ogling him.

He smiles, takes a step forward, and bends over to place a kiss on my lips.

"Hello, Angel!"

"Hi," I almost whisper back.

"So, I take it you're driving?" He nods to my position behind the wheel.

"Yep, do you mind?"

"Nope, I trust you."

"You do? I mean it's great you do, but *really*?"

"I don't have any reason not to."

"I guess you could say that, but do you have any reason *to*?"

"Do *you* need a reason to trust me?"

"Yes... No... I don't know. That depends I guess."

I can't help but think we're talking about something bigger again. How does he do that? It's strange he would even raise such a serious topic, *trust*. Why point out the weakness in our relationship when, since we're just having casual fun anyway, we could simply pretend it doesn't exist? It's not like this is serious for him. It's just a short-lived vacation romance.

My thoughts are interrupted when he lowers to kiss my forehead. The gesture so simple, yet every time, it feels extremely intimate. His lips linger there just a second longer than usual, and I close my eyes and inhale his scent. He smelled like ocean and sun before, but now that scent is replaced with something fresh, masculine, with a hint of spice. It's familiar, but more intense.

He lifts his lips and looks at me, my eyes still closed. I'm caught in a blissful moment of daydreaming. He chuckles softly and pecks my forehead gently one more time, as if to wake me up.

My eyes fly open, and I yelp when I realize I've been caught.

"You're like a dream angel, you know that? One minute you're here, and the next, you're in your own dreamland."

"Sorry, I got carried away."

"It's ok, I'm used to it, and I think it's pretty cute."

He walks around the car and gets in.

"Want me to lead you or would you prefer the GPS?"

"Lead the way, mister!"

"With pleasure!"

We spend the next half hour driving, laughing, and talking about everything and nothing. I feel so at ease around him, not planning what to say next, not worrying what he's going to think, not paying attention to how I look, not obsessing over what impression he's going to get. It's amazing and so unbelievable.

We arrive and park the car. I put the top back up, and we walk out of the parking garage tower.

He gives me a walking tour of Lincoln Avenue, around the small shops, cafes, and restaurants. We settle down in one of the small South American restaurants that have tables along the sidewalk. It's decorated in orange colors, small tables topped with candles. The sun has set, making the whole scene incredibly romantic. I look over the menu, searching for something interesting and not too big.

"Want a suggestion?" Alex asks, noticing my indecision.

"Tell me, everything seems delicious, but I want something light."

"Fish. Baked, seared, or even raw if you don't mind it."

"Well, I like sushi, but I'm not sure how it's done outside of Japanese cuisine."

"Let's get a couple of different ceviche dishes and you can pick the one you like."

"What's ceviche?"

"In short, fish and other seafood in lime juice, topped with a variety of things, like cilantro, mango, bell peppers, tomatoes, or pineapples. Whatever you can think of. Every place does them differently, but they are great. Best of all, they use local fish that was just caught."

"Sounds delicious. I'm salivating already. What are you drinking?"

"Mojito, you?"

"I was just thinking the same." I wink at him.

"We think alike a lot."

He is smiling at me, and I have the biggest urge to kiss him. I wrap my hand around his neck and pull him to me, placing a deep kiss on his lips. He kisses me back, taking my other hand in his and running circles with his thumb.

The waitress arrives to take our order. Alex goes over the dishes and drinks with her, all the while holding my hand. The girl is ogling him openly, her eyes lingering around the open buttons of his shirt. I feel rather possessive of Alex, wanting to put my claim on him, let her know he is with me, off limits. He seems completely oblivious to her looks and simply holds my hand in his, gently rubbing it with his thumb. I look at him and realize he's not even remotely interested in this girl. Regardless of her hot body and seeming availability, he simply does not care. He's not pretending, not trying to look disinterested while sneaking a look at her. He's here with me and that's all that matters. As soon as he finishes ordering, his eyes are on mine again. One look and I forget all the worries I just had. Amazing!

We chat a while, waiting for the food to arrive. Our drinks come first, and Alex raises a toast.

"To you, my dream angel!"

I smile and click glasses with him. Sipping the mojito, I feel alcohol spreading through my body. I realize I did not eat anything today and driving back might be a problem.

"So, do you like convertibles?" This simple question makes his head fly up in surprise.

"Why? Do you want to know what I drive?" A cautious look crosses his face, but vanishes before I have the chance to get a good look.

"Not really, why? I was just wondering if you would like to drive back?"

The smallest wrinkles around his eyes and forehead relax, and he smiles back.

"Sure, I'd love to get a chance to drive your Audi."

I wonder what made him look tense. What could he be worried about? Maybe he had an accident, or something like that. I decide to not raise the subject again, since it clearly makes him uneasy.

As we finish dinner, Alex slips his credit card to the waitress before I have a chance to protest. He looks determined and I realize arguing is useless.

"Would you like to go for a walk?"

"Yeah, sure, I'd love to."

My hand is in his, my small palm fitting perfectly in his masculine one. We wander the small streets, making our way to Ocean Drive, where the party is on. Trying to move with the crowds of people, we soon give up and cross the street to walk along the beach walkway. There, the crowd is thinner, and the smell of the ocean is stronger. I can even hear the waves. Alex stops me and with a swift lift, sits me up on the stone pillar half-wall separating the beach sand from the walkway. He gently squeezes my calves and unties the straps of one sandal, then the other, taking them off completely. I look at him in surprise, not knowing what to expect next but too excited to protest. His hands slide from my ankles up to my knees, continuing their trail on the sides of my thighs. I try to push my knees together to relieve some of the tension he's building, but Alex is standing right against the pillars. Our lips touch softly, breaths exchanged. My head falls back with Alex leaning further into me, his hands supporting me. My legs wrap around his as he intensifies the kiss, pushing me further back. My heart races with both arousal and fear of falling over the pillar. Legs crossed, I lace my arms under Alex's elbows and hold on tight, our bodies pushed together, hearts beating against each other. We kiss for minutes, consuming each other, learning each other's taste and curves, my hands gliding over Alex's muscular back, remembering every ridge and valley. His fingers skim my thighs, whispery touches igniting a spark deep inside my core. He doesn't even get close to the lace of my underwear, which is soaking wet by now. His passionate kiss and a hint of his touch are enough to make me a hot, wet mess.

I yelp as he leans even further into me.

"Remember, I've got you, always!" His words vibrate against my lips.

I have no comeback for this but to kiss him again while grasping him tightly.

He straightens up, pulling me alongside. I loosen my embrace now that my body is no longer inclined over the pillar. Alex's hands travel all the way up to my cheeks, skimming my jawline and sending a flurry of goosebumps all the way to my bare toes.

"You are an angel. My sweet angel." His eyes penetrate deep into my soul, surely seeing things that are hidden for a reason. I break the eye contact, unable to hold the intensity of his gaze.

"Believe me, I might be sweet, but I'm not an angel." I look at my entwined fingers resting on my lap. He lifts my chin up, and I'm faced with the clearness of his blues.

"To me, you most definitely are. In more ways than you can imagine." Something very vulnerable flashes in his eyes, but I don't get a chance to look any closer. His lips cover mine in the softest kiss, filled with tenderness.

"I have a special place I'd like to take you." His smile is contagious, with a hint of mischief in it. I feel excitement bubbling up inside. I can't believe how easy it is to be with Alex. No pressure, no judgement, no contempt. A girl could get used to this.

Alex settles down next to me, removes his shoes, and rolls his jeans up to just below his knees. Before I realize what's going on, he lifts me in his arms and carries to the beach, our shoes dangling by the laces in his right hand. Once we're by the water, he keeps walking along the shore. I squeal and beg to be put down.

Finally, he relents. My feet find solid ground and the cool water washes around them. The beach is dark, lit only by the full moon hanging over the ocean. I raise on my tip toes and kiss his cheek.

"This is so romantic. Thank you!"

"I wanted to take you away from the craziness of the tourists, but I wasn't sure if you minded getting all messy in the sand. I was ready to carry you along the shore."

"I'm not that high-maintenance." I give him a raised brow for the assumption.

"I don't mind the sand, and I can't believe you'd carry me."

"It's not such a long walk. This place is a little farther down the beach."

"Ok, great! I love the water by the way. Too bad it's dark and I can't see any shells."

"You like them, don't you?" Alex says with amusement.

"Ever since I was a little girl. I can't get enough."

"We'll collect some tomorrow."

We walk along the shore, holding hands and talking. The wind carries echoes of faint music from the distance. A few minutes later, we turn right and walk up the shore to an outside restaurant/lounge. There are tables in the back, cabanas all along the perimeter, and huge white beds in the middle of the grounds. Only a few tables and a cabana across from us are occupied. The whole place looks surreal, unbelievably peaceful for such a huge venue just minutes from all the nightlife. The soft music is playing all around now, invisible speakers covering every corner.

"It is so serene. I would have never thought it was possible in the middle of the South Beach chaos."

"Yeah, I know. It's just not their hottest night. You should see what goes on here on Sundays and during special parties. This place is ripped to pieces. I like it both ways, though."

"Are we going to get a table?"

"Oh no, we're going to settle in one of the cabanas, if you don't mind." His lopsided smile screams mischief. I'm buzzing with aftereffects of the mojito, or maybe it's my body's reaction to Alex. His proximity and anticipation of what's coming make me hot in all the wrong places.

"Sounds good to me. I could use some relaxing time," I say, as nonchalantly as I can master. Luckily Alex isn't watching my face—the one he seems to be able to read so well.

"That was precisely the plan." His hand wraps around mine, pulling softly as he leads the way.

We walk around and decide on a cabana tucked away behind a leafy palm tree. The three other sides are covered with white linens that fly in the wind. This place is the epitome of romantic. I can't believe that in the many times I'd come to Miami, I'd never heard of it before.

The bed of the cabana is raised, and I'm trying to figure out the best way to climb it gracefully. Alex sees me contemplating the ascent and without asking, just grabs my waist and lifts me up and on top of the bed. I yelp in excitement and push myself further along the mattress and against the huge pillows that line the sides.

A waitress comes by and Alex orders another mojito for me and a sparkling water for himself. I am definitely not driving today.

He settles next to me and relaxes back against the pillows, snaking his arm around my waist and pulling me to him. I relax against his side, resting my head on his chest. Neither of us says anything. The silence is comforting, and the proximity of our bodies is even more enjoyable. We both seem to revel in the here and now. I have no expectations. I just want to live in this moment forever, with this man next to me, shielding me from the world. When I'm with him, nothing else seems to matter. I feel like a different person. So much for taking time off to find myself...

Our drinks arrive and interrupt the silence. The mojito here is even better than the one in the restaurant. The tall glass is full of mint that gives off an unmistakable aroma.

"Mmm, I love it." I inhale the minty scent again and take another sip.

Alex's gentle lips find their way to mine. I feel their heat against the chillness of my mouth. The icy coldness and minty rum flavor still linger on my tongue. Alex groans and deepens the kiss, taking possessive charge of it. I melt in his touch. My mouth, my muscles, my mind, everything wants to submit to the desire ignited by this one mysterious man.

We kiss for minutes, slowing down, breathing each other in and resuming the dance of our tongues all over again.

At some point we resume talking in a quiet whisper, as if we're sharing our secrets, even though we're talking about nothing in particular.

Come to think of it, I don't even know his last name, and I doubt he knows mine. We've managed to spend some time together, and have mind-blowing sex a handful of times, but we don't even know each other's last name.

Yet, I think he understands me better than my fiancée or my own parents. He seems to sense me, read right through me, and anticipate my every wish.

In turn, I see his mood changes, notice the shade his eyes lighten when he's happy, darken when he's aroused, and go grayish when he's worried. I see his jaw tense, and I know not to push the subject.

We seem to have our own lives, secrets we aren't ready to reveal, yet we find peace in each other's company. Maybe this is all a facade. Just an illusion we like to believe.

We don't know much about each other, and might be seeing what we want to see. What if we revealed everything? What if he knew what was beneath the surface of this carefree girl he sees in Miami? Would he want to deal with my issues? Why bother? He can have any girl he wants, so why would he choose one with baggage?

My face must be revealing my feelings once again. I feel him run his fingers along my cheek, his thumb gliding across my forehead.

"I know this is none of my business, but I just wanted you to know if there is anything I can do for you, please tell me. I hate to see this struggle on your face. You look so sad sometimes." He holds my gaze and lifts my hand to his lips for a kiss.

"I'm sorry, I don't mean to ruin the moment. I just have a lot on my mind. I came to Florida to sort through my life, to figure things out. Then I met you, and I'm having the most fun I've had in years. So, every now and then I revert back to trying to sort through things. I'm not doing it on purpose, it just happens and I can't help it." I give him an apologetic look.

"Can you talk about it? What's eating at you?" There is no curiosity, just compassion in his look.

"I'd rather not, if you don't mind."

"I understand, I can relate to that." His voice is quiet, full of meaning, without giving anything away.

Our fingers are interlaced and we keep that connection, spending the rest of the night talking and kissing, hidden away in the cabana. At some point things get so hot we almost have sex right there. We're both panting and tugging on each other's clothes. I want him so badly, yet I can't do it out in public, even if it *is* dark. He pulls me onto his lap and kisses my neck and bare shoulders. I marvel in his kisses, wishing for more but restraining my desires. Then his hand crawls under the hem of my dress, and I gasp in surprise.

"Not here, no, no, no!" I protest in a hurried, hushed voice.

"Shhh." His lips swallow my protest, and I open my mouth completely, submitting to him and my desire.

His fingers slide up to the lace of my thong and make contact with the soaking fabric.

"You are so wet. All for me." I can't speak, just gasping for air and nodding shyly.

His strong, skilled fingers push the lace to the side and brush against my lips. A quiver runs through my body, and I tug my hand along his back, clawing at it.

His fingers, slick with my moisture, make their way into my folds and rub the sensitive bud. I moan into his mouth and pull his hair to have a deeper kiss that will quiet my moans.

He runs the tiniest circles around my clit, but I'm so wound up, I feel the orgasm approaching. I kiss him deeper and more possessively, moaning into his mouth. The thrill of being caught escalates my excitement. Few moments later I feel on edge.

The orgasm builds and heat spreads over my body. I curl in his lap, trying to control myself. It's a lost battle. The feeling is so strong, I'm drowning in it. As the sensations build up, his fingers plunge deep inside of me, rubbing the perfect spot and sending me over the edge. A cry escapes my mouth and is swallowed by his kiss. I'm shaking and clawing and pulling on him, my body writhing against his. He slows down and moves his fingers inside of me slowly, as if calming me down from the inside, and I can breathe again.

I look up in his eyes and see them full of lust, dilated to the point where I barely see the blues.

"You are so sexy when you come. I love watching you, love knowing I caused that." His voice is hoarse, barely above whisper.

"That was earth-shattering! Let's get back home, I want to return the favor."

"You seem to object to the public places." That lopsided smile is permanently in place now.

"I've never done anything like that in public, well, except for just now." Red creeps up my cheeks.

"This was your first time, huh?" His eyes sparkle.

"Yes, indeed."

"Well, let's not stop at what we have accomplished so far." His fingers are still circling in a slow, hypnotizing motion deep inside of me.

"What do you mean?" I whisper breathily, tucking my face in the crook of his neck, floating in the cloud of my post-orgasmic haze.

He says nothing, just works his fingers a little faster, as if waking me up. I'm afraid to even think of what he means by not stopping now. My heart starts pumping so fast, it's ready to jump out of my chest.

He slowly pulls his fingers out of me, sliding them over my swollen clit. A shudder runs through my whole body. I lift my head just in time to see him lick the moisture away from them. Our eyes meet and he presses a wet finger to my bottom lip. I open my mouth and suck it in, swirling my tongue around it. I taste myself on his fingers, the raw pleasure of just minutes ago assaulting my senses.

He gently takes my hand and places it over the bulge in his jeans, his erection pushing hard against the material.

I feel moisture pool between my legs, my senses on overdrive. The bulge I'm rubbing with my palm is the last straw. He groans and pinches his eyes shut. I marvel at the effect I have on him. I want to shatter his control, rip it to shreds, and own it. I hope I won't regret my transgressions in the morning.

I unzip his fly and fumble with the belt. As soon as I reach his cock, I feel it twitching in my hand. I grasp it and push down, baring his glistering head. My hair is falling down around my face, creating a curtain that hides me and his cock from the world around. I'm glad it's there. I don't think I'm ready to be watched performing oral sex out in the open. He must sense my insecurity, and doesn't try to pull it back.

My lips are on him, kissing, licking, running my tongue up and down the length of his cock. I put the tip in my mouth and suck gently, feeling him stiffen under my touch, his breathing haltering. His cock grows even harder in my hand, twitching with every touch of my lips. In one deep plunge, I cover most of him with my lips, pushing the head deep down my throat. Alex groans loudly while I try not to gag, pulling out, only to take him back in even deeper. I want to please him, to make him come the way he did for me. A few more strokes and I feel him becoming steel-hard in my mouth. He is close and is trying to push me away.
"I'm close, so close, you don't have to..."

I suck him for my dear life, feeling tears collecting in my eyes.
Then he bursts, hot liquid running down my throat. I suck relentlessly, feeling my lips go numb but determined to get every last bit of him, as if this is

my only water in the desert. When he seems to be empty, I slow down and let him out of my mouth with a few lapping licks of my tongue.

I am physically spent and breathless. Alex makes quick work of righting his jeans. He leans over me and kisses me gently, the tips of our noses rubbing against each other.

"This was amazing. I never thought you had this in you." There is no mischief in his eyes now, just pure awe.

I blush and kiss him again. Surprising, I never thought I had this in me either. He brings out sides of me I wasn't even aware are there. With him, it's like I'm coming to life.

Chapter 10

We walk back along the beach, hand in hand. As earlier, the silence is comforting. I replay the events of this evening in my mind. Where did this boldness come from? Alex? Lust? Alcohol? A mix of the three? Either way, I feel no regrets. This is such new and forbidden territory for me.

When we get to the parking lot, I hand Alex the keys. He walks me to the passenger side, opens the door, and plants me in the car with such care, as though I'm a crystal vase. Then he closes the door and walks around to sit behind the wheel. The top is lowered, and we are ready to go.

I relax back against the leather seats and feel my lids getting heavy. The breeze blows in my face, and I close my eyes. I feel like I'm being carried by wind, high up in the sky, riding a cloud.

My body is weightless. Light kisses are covering my face, and I open my eyes. Alex is smiling at me. I feel disoriented for a moment.

"Wake up, Angel, we're just a stoplight away."

"I was dreaming. I was flying." I whisper as I try to push the sleep away.

"I told you, you are a lot like an angel. My angel." The last two words are pronounced with such emotion in his voice that I do not dare protest, only comment.

"Angels do good deeds and save people. I'm the opposite, I do well-calculated business and I'm lost, how can I save anyone?" I'm whispering half asleep.

"You are; you just don't know it. My angel." Again, the last two words are pronounced with such emotion, his voice soft, barely a whisper. I don't know if he really said it, or if it was a dream.

I open my eyes as I'm being lifted from the car by Alex's strong arms. He cradles me and holds me up. I walk unsteadily, then I'm lifted in his arms as soon as we step into the empty elevator.

Once we reach my door, I blindly search through my purse for the card key and pass it to Alex. He slides it inside the lock and pushes the door open.

We step into the cool air of my condo. Alex walks to the bedroom and puts me down on the bed. He undresses me, starting with untying the laces at my ankles. Step by step, he frees me of all my clothing. I'm aware of his hands on me, and his eyes devouring my body, but I have no strength left. I simply submit to his powerful arms and soon find myself stark naked and under the covers. The bed feels cool and soft, cloud-like, and I start falling back asleep, returning to my flying dream. Then the loss of his touch on my body sends me into panic, and I scream his name in desperation.

"Alex!" He is there in a heartbeat, cradling me with his gentle touch, kissing my forehead.

"I'm here." He whispers softly in my ear.

I feel stupid, I'm almost ready to cry. Why do I feel this way? I can't think now, I can only feel that I need him, I can't lose him.
I manage to croak.

"Don't leave, please." He hugs me tight and kisses gently.

"I won't, I promise. Let me just take off my clothes and I'll be right there."

I lose his touch again and turn my attention to

listening to him undress, to making sure he isn't leaving. I'm so tired, the sex, alcohol, and sun taking a huge toll on my body. Then I feel him climbing into bed and pressing his strong body against mine.

"You're back, don't ever leave me." My words are barely audible, and as I relax against him, I fall asleep.

I dream of flying in the wind, and of the softest clouds holding me up in the sky. Then, in my mind's eye, the clouds begin to form a face—a real face. The expressions on the face are flipping one after another: happy, smiling, sad, sexy, dreamy, thoughtful, pained, caring, loving. I keep eye contact through this whirlwind of emotions, and share them all. This face belongs to Alex, and I realize I could never grow tired of looking at it. I want to learn everything about him, the good and the bad. I want to share his happiness and sadness, and in turn, share mine with him. I dream of the feeling of unity, being with someone, being myself, being whole.

The dreams return throughout the night. I wake to his hands holding me gently, and I fall back asleep. This night is unlike any other I've had in my life. I dread the morning as it approaches and the sky lights up with the first rays of the rising sun. But deep inside, I feel calm and safe. I nuzzle back into Alex's chest and return to sleep. This time, it's a deep sleep that takes me well into the late morning.

Chapter 11

I wake to the smell of coffee and a room filled with sunshine. It must be after ten for sure, as the sun is already high above the ocean. I'm alone in the bed, wrapped in layers of thin white sheets. I get up, picking up the loose ends, and move in the direction of the aroma. Making a quick stop in the bathroom, I pass the living room and head to the kitchen. Alex is behind the counter, looking deliciously fresh in just his jeans. He looks up and smiles.

"Hello, sleepy angel!"

"Morning. What time is it? When did you get up?"

"It's around eleven. I've been up for a while, working from my phone, trying to get as much done as I could. There's still stuff I have to finish."

Then it hits me: it's Monday. He needs to work, and I need to call the office and check on things as well. Our weekend affair is over, welcome back to reality. The dreams, they were just that, dreams. We have our own lives to live.

I force a smile onto my face, hoping he missed the kaleidoscope of emotions before it—emotions he inexplicably reads so well. Too late! As usual, he is on top of his game.

"Hey now, what's with the look? I know nobody likes Mondays, but it seems you hate them." His voice is playful, yet it rings with cautious notes.

"Do you want to pretend it's still Sunday? I can stay and take you to the beach, and lunch, and shopping, and whatever else there is to do on Sundays." He lifts my chin up and searches my eyes.

So we'll pretend it's Sunday, and then what? Monday still comes next. I have to let him go. I can't let myself get attached to him. I'm getting lost in him. There is no *me* again. I'm trying to build another *us*. I am leaving in a couple of weeks. Time is running out.

"No, it's ok, go on to work, do your stuff. I have to call the office myself, and I have no idea how long it will take." I do my best to sound collected and hide the turmoil going on inside. For a change, it works.

"Ok, how about I call you when I'm done and we get together?"
"You don't have to do that. I realize this is not a vacation for you, and you have to get back to your life." Or maybe he doesn't.

"I know I don't have to, I want to. Remember, I said you could see me again if you simply wanted to. I meant it. If you want to, then you will see me again, and again, and again." His eyes hold mine.

I nod before I even have time to consider. My mind screams stay away, but my heart begs for more. More of this simple human interaction, more of the happy times we seem to have together.

I'm walking on thin ice. I'm attracted to him, so how do I manage to keep from getting hurt, given I'm leaving soon? I guess it's a chance I have to take. Suddenly, I understand the metaphor of a moth flying too close to the flame all too well.

He kisses my forehead again, a simple show of affection I'm now accustomed to. Every time I have troubling thoughts, he literally kisses them away. These moments feel incredibly intimate. I take his face in my palms and smile.

"I want to."

"Then you will. It's that simple." He punctuates his promise with a kiss.

Strong arms lift me up and place me on the counter top. I'm still wrapped in layers of sheets. Handing me a cup of coffee, Alex turns to the stove and I notice he's made eggs and toast. This is awesome. I try to remember the last time someone made me hot breakfast. It's been about a decade, for sure. Seems like an eternity, considering I'm only 27.

"I didn't know you cooked." What else don't I know?

"I've been living on my own since I was pretty young. Pizza and take-out get old pretty quickly, so I learned. I like good food. Maybe one day I'll cook a dinner for you, some fish or shrimp, with a nice sauce and a good wine to pair with it." Who would have thought? Then again, there's still so much I don't know.

"Wow! Sounds fancy. I can't cook too much, just a few quick dishes, maybe some salads. I never had proper culinary training. My mother doesn't cook at all; we've always had a person living with us." My mom never even ate breakfast in the kitchen. All her food was served in the dining room.

"Like a housekeeper?" He sounds surprised, as if I don't pass for a kid raised wealthy, with stuck-up parents.

"Yeah, something like that. When I was little we also had a live-in nanny who took care of me. Then I grew up, and my mom let her go."

I remember my nanny, Sophia, and how she used to be the closest thing I had to an affectionate mother. My own never took any time to spend cuddling with me, opting instead for regular lectures about what a real lady should and should not do. I can still hear her condescending tone. It hasn't changed, all these years later.

"You loved her, didn't you?" I'm confused for seconds, looking at him in question.

"Your nanny." His words sound tender, a perfect match for the way I feel about Sophia.

"Yes, we were incredibly close. She was like a mix of a mother and a grandmother to me. My mom isn't

127

big on affection." I sigh forlornly. Nothing I can do about it now, or could have done in the past, regardless how hard I tried.

"Why did your mom let her go?" There is curiosity mixed with surprise in his voice—more proof her decision made no sense. I always thought so too, but never argued with her logic.

"She thought it was improper to have such a close bond with hired help, as she put it." Alex eyes go wide, but he stays silent, letting me finish.

"I think I was depressed for a year after that. She never let me see her again. I can't even imagine what Sophia must have thought about me. She put her heart and soul into me, and never once was I allowed to call her, not even on holidays. Never." I play with the folds of the white sheet wrapped around me to avoid looking at Alex. Unshed tears are burning behind my eyes. I was never allowed to cry then, and I am not going to cry now.

"Wow! Your mom is an interesting character."

"To say the least."

"Surprisingly, I can somewhat relate to this. I spent my time in private boarding schools, then colleges and dorms. I missed out on the warm family ties and domestic upbringing."

Now a shadow runs through his face, and I know we have come upon a sensitive topic for both of us. Most of our conversations yesterday were lighthearted and didn't touch on any sensitive issues. I try to lighten the mood a little.

"And look how well you turned out, Mr. I-can-cook-and-do-everything-myself!" A playful smile and a wink finish the job, his face relaxing a bit.

"Well, huh? You think I turned out pretty well? You aren't so bad yourself." The lopsided smile and mischievous eyes are back.

"Yeah, I think so. Whereas you think I'm *not bad*, huh? So, it's not that I'm good or great, just not so bad." I tease him for his word choice.

"Well, I'd have to see you in action in the kitchen first, before I could give my final assessment..."

"In action?" It's clearly flirtatious innuendo. Alex chuckles softly and takes two steps in my direction. Narrow hips wedge between my knees, and I spread them just enough to make room for him.

"Let's see some action." Alex whispers softly, before swiping his lips gently against mine. I wrap my arms around his neck and deepen the kiss, completely ignoring my falling sheets. Our bare chests touch, and I feel momentarily aroused. His fingers trace along my bare back, sending shivers down to my toes. My fingers are tugging the wavy locks of his hair. I push against his chest to leave no space between us. Then I break the kiss.

"Didn't you cook me breakfast?" I'm teasing him now, rubbing my nipple against his bare chest. His eyes are glued to our skin-to-skin connection.

"It can wait, first I'm going to have my desert, Angel-cake."

His lips are back on mine, fingers teasing my nipples into hard peaks. A moan escapes my mouth and I spread my legs wider to let him in closer.
He trails wet kisses down my neckline and sucks on my already-hard nipples, biting down on them gently. My head rolls back, and I put my arms behind me to support myself. My chest pushes further into his face, and he buries himself between my heavy breasts, pushing them together with both hands.

Slowly kissing his way down, he makes it to my hips; they're wrapped in layers of sheets. I wiggle my butt in an effort to free myself from them. Alex lifts me up and off the counter. The sheets pool at our feet with a whisper, and I'm stark naked. Planting me back on the kitchen counter and spreading my legs wide, he pushes me to lean back on my elbows, and I watch his lips trail kisses to my center. He blows a warm breath of air, and I shudder inside in anticipation of his delicious lips on me. He's teasing me, using the very tip of his tongue to run a slow circle around my clit. I shake and release a loud whimper.

"Are you wet for me?"

"Why don't you check?"

"I will, in a minute."

Alex pulls his face away and blows more air at my core, this time with more force, so it comes out chilly. I tremble, and he puts his hands over the round globes of my butt to hold me in place. Then in one rapid move he drops his lips on me and sucks my already-too-sensitive nub fiercely. I'm screaming his name loudly now. His strong hands keep my body from jerking, and I beg for more.

I'm getting close, and he feels it. His sucking slows just a bit, and I relax and get frustrated all at once.

"Don't stop, please!"

"What would you like me to do?" His voice vibrates against me, sending small shockwaves.

"Please, go on. Please!"

"Tell me more."

"Please kiss me again." I'm ready to start begging and not even ashamed of it.

"Do you want me to kiss you like this?" He runs his lips along my swollen folds.

"Or would you like me to suck you?" His mouth is back on my nub, sucking it hard into his mouth.

I scream and can barely hold up on my elbows, but it's not enough to make me come.

I look at his mouth on me, and the view is amazing. He looks up again.

"What would you like? More kisses?" He is playing with me, and I can barely contain myself.

"Please make me come with your mouth, please," I'm begging for release now, my whole body in tight coils, ready to explode.

"Since you're asking so nicely." He puts his hand flat on my stomach and glides it up, pushing my back flat on the counter top. I relax and spread my legs wider for him.

"Put your legs on my shoulders." I oblige immediately.

Alex lowers his head down, out of my line of sight, and I tremble in anticipation of his lips.

His fingers plunge deeply into me as his mouth crashes down. I scream and instinctively buck my hips up. The sensational overload takes me to the edge, and I cry out.

"More, more, don't stop, I'm so close, so close."

He keeps the frantic pace, and I feel my walls clenching around his fingers. The orgasm is so strong, I'm drowning in it. Gasping for air, I scream his name over and over, until I have no more energy. Alex slows down gradually to let me ride out the last wave. I am spent, on the counter top, unable to lift a single limb. Alex gently cradles me in his arms and carries me to the sofa while kissing my mouth ever so lightly.

We settle onto the luxury leather and I'm on his lap, naked and exhausted. He continues to kiss me while I regain my senses. I taste myself on his lips, caressing his mouth. My limbs are soft and boneless.

Slowly my senses return, and I'm no longer dizzy. I kiss him harder, still tasting myself all over his mouth, and whisper into the kiss.

"That was unbelievable."

He chuckles softly and kisses me, exploring my curves with his hands.

I lift up to straddle him and go for his belt. Never mind that I just came, I want him again, and even more than before. He helps me out and lifts his hips to push the jeans down.

I lower myself, teasing him right at my entrance, circling my hips and rubbing my nub against his swollen head. He groans louder and gets a stronger hold on my hips, lifting me up just enough to enter.

"Easy, easy, not so soon," I laugh and say into his kiss as I lick his lower lip.

"You're driving me crazy. I'm going to fuck you so hard now, you'll scream."

"How about we start really slow? I want to feel you inside of me."

I look straight into his eyes as I lower myself down, feeling Alex bury himself inside of me. The moment is so intense, neither one of us dares to break the eye contact. Once I sit on his lap, I push down a bit more to leave no space between us, to take all of him in as deep as I can. I feel this connection, although purely physical at the moment, start to transform into something new. We are drowning in each other's eyes. I make the tiniest of circles with my hips, feeling him deep in my core. In this moment, we are one being, breathing as one, feeling as one. Slowly, we find our own, unhurried rhythm, and begin to move in complete unison, as if dancing.
I hug him closer and our chests are pushed together. My lips are on his, noses touching, while our eyes remain locked. I feel Alex's hands gripping me tighter as we continue our slow, torturous pace.

Even this slight friction starts to build with undeniable force inside of me. I clench my inner walls tighter as I strive to prolong this moment of pure bliss between us.

"You are incredible, breathtaking. You are my precious Angel." Alex's words are a faint whisper against my lips, but I feel the deepest sincerity in them.

"Alex, oh Alex..."

I don't know where it came from, but I have the deepest sense I belong with him. Moreover, I feel a claim to him; he is mine. I couldn't bear losing him, or sharing him with anyone. Oh god, my fear is being realized. I'm falling for the wrong guy, again. But it feels unbelievable. I'm alive again. So be it. I'll fall down the rabbit hole.

I guess another whirlwind of emotions goes through my face. Alex breaks eye contact to plant the softest and gentlest kiss on my forehead. I melt at the touch of his lips and lift my chin up, offering a kiss. Our mouths lock, and the intensity of the kiss grows by the second. We are devouring each other shamelessly, moaning and groaning into each other. His strong arms guide me around his cock faster as he lifts his hips with more force to meet my every thrust. Gone are the gentle touches, replaced by pure, raw desire that is uncontainable. Our pace is frantic, our moves quick and sharp.

Lifting up, I plunge back down with force and am met by his raised hips, stroke for stroke. He is filling the deepest parts of me, penetrating so far, to the virgin parts of my inner core that seem to never have been touched by anyone. I am oversensitive, my previous orgasm putting me on the edge, making me tremble with the onslaught of another one approaching and rendering me barely able to control myself, yet afraid to let go.

I feel him shaking underneath me, and I know he must be struggling the same way I am. I want to prolong the moment, and in an effort to do so, I try to slow down, looking him straight in the eyes. He understands without words. My pleading gaze is enough. We are slowing down, eyes locked, embracing the moment.

I feel him buried deep inside and clench my muscles around his length in a final, hopeless attempt to take control of my body. He releases a deep breath he must have been holding and pushes me deeper against himself.

"I want you, I can't slow down. Move with me, dance with me."

He takes his hands off my hips and we press our palms together, fingers interlaced. I lift my hips and sway lightly from side to side, then I lower them down again and grind against him. We're moving in complete unison, like we've been doing this our entire lives. Our tempo increases slowly, and soon enough, we're going at it again. I watch his cock pull out of me almost all the way, only to be swallowed right back in.

Soon, there's no more prolonging the inevitable. With each thrust the orgasm unravels deep in my core, sending tingling sensations across my whole body.

I get louder and louder, screaming Alex's name over and over. My head keeps falling back, eyes rolling, but I try hard to keep them locked on Alex's.

"Look at me, Angel!" My head jerks up again and I look him straight in the eye.

"My Angel!"

"Yours!"

The orgasm sends an electric current traversing our bodies, our hands still locked together in a white-knuckled hold. The last wave passes through my body, and I'm jelly in his hands. Collapsing over his chest, I hide my face in the nook of his neck and place a wet kiss on his pulsing vein. Alex wraps one of his arms around my shoulders, while the other one snakes around my waist. I feel completely engulfed in him. I feel safe. Two loose pieces of a puzzle have finally fallen into place.

He pulls me closer and I fully relax against his muscular chest, resting my head on his shoulder, hugging my arms around his neck, and inhaling his scent—the one I found so arousing from the very first time I breathed it in. Now, it is also deeply familiar. I would recognize it unmistakably among dozens of others.

His fingers draw lazy circles along my lower back while I run mine through his hair. We enjoy the silence, neither of us wanting to break the fragile bond that seems to be building between us. Our breaths come in unison, in and out, two parts of one whole.

A phone call comes from somewhere close, and I

don't recall the ringtone. Alex stirs under me slightly and relaxes back.

"Are you going to get it?"

"Nope, I'll call back later."

Silence fills the room again, only to be broken by what I assume is the chime of a voicemail. Alex seems not to care.

The phone starts ringing again. This time it's a different tone, one that gets Alex's attention immediately.

"Sorry, I think I better take it."

I lift up to let him out. Once he's on his feet, he makes a beeline to the kitchen and grabs his phone there. As my body loses contact with his, I start shivering and feel overexposed and self-conscious. Wrapping myself in a throw that was thankfully right beside me on the opposite armrest, I look at Alex.

The phone is pushed to his ear as he looks straight ahead. His facial expression is giving nothing away, except his jaws seem to clench tightly together. I assume whoever is on the other line is not bearing any good news. Alex does not utter a single word, just keeps listening.

"Ok, I'll be there." He disconnects the call and walks around to the living room. Pulling on his jeans, he finally makes eye contact with me.

"I'm sorry, Angel. I have to go. Now."

Something about him is different, distant, as if there is a wall being erected between us. I don't know what it is. I don't dare asking him if he's coming back to see me again. It would break me if he said no right to my face. I just sit there and watch him. Alex takes his shirt from one of the dining chairs and puts it on. After finishing righting his clothes, he stops in front of me and leans over to kiss my forehead. He plants his lips right along the small vein that seems to give me away each time. His kiss is as gentle and intimate as I remember it.

"I don't know how long I'll be. I'll see you as soon as I deal with this situation. If you need me, just text the number I left on the countertop."

Alex lifts my face to him and kisses my lips gently. No hot passion or lust, just a tender kiss. I look into his eyes and see something that wasn't there before. From dark blues flooded with lust and passion, they are icy cold now.

I nod and try not to break down in tears. I'm not sure what has happened. I've never seen him like this, and it's somewhat frightening. The glare sends shivers through my whole body.

"Have some fun while I'm gone. Go by the beach, maybe shop later. Just relax and enjoy yourself, ok?"

I nod again and he pecks my lips before heading straight to the door.

Once it closes behind him, the tears start falling uncontrollably from my eyes. I feel lost, and I can't even understand why.

I make it to the bathroom, vision blurred by tears, and step under the hot shower. I let the water run down my body, standing there with my eyes closed, trying to pull myself together. Is this what it's going to feel like when I have to put actual distance between us and go back to Chicago? Or will it be worse?

I let the water wash away my tears, regaining strength in process.

I came to Miami to rediscover myself, to find a new path for my life, but instead I'm a mess. I fell for the first guy I saw, and now I'm lost without him.

I have to learn to be strong for myself, find my own way.

I laugh at the feeling I woke up with. Dreaming of Alex all night left me high in the sky. Reality is far from euphoric.

I calm down and step out of the shower with a resolve to take matters into my own hands. I make no long-term plans or promises to myself. I'm simply going to go right back to where I started and focus on me, making sure to enjoy the rest of my time here to the fullest.

First things first, I need to eat. Stepping into the kitchen, I'm immediately assaulted by remnants of Alex's presence. The coffee he made for me is cold now, so I pour it down the sink and make myself another cup. The toast is salvageable, and I bite into it.

The calls to the office are next. I check my email first, to make sure I haven't missed anything. To my delight there is nothing urgent there. Then I call my assistant, Kelly. Her quick update confirms everything is running smoothly. I exhale with relief. The most dreadful call, the one to my father, won't be needed.

It's already past one in the afternoon by the time I wrap up. The sun is high and hot. Skipping the beach would be wise, considering I nearly burned the other day. I change into my yoga clothes and head straight to the studio I saw nearby, hoping they'll have a class taking place.

Chapter 12

It turns out they do indeed have a class, and I make it right on time. I prepay quickly, refusing to purchase a membership just yet.

The practice is intense, but fun. For the next ninety minutes, I completely forget all my worries. The instructor is a young lady, probably around my age. She is beautiful, yet seems completely oblivious of her looks. Being a mid-height brunette, I have a soft spot for tall blonds. They always remind me of the picture-perfect beauty. That's what this girl is. Slim and toned all over, with golden skin and perfectly chiseled features.

As I'm collecting my things after class and getting ready to leave the studio, she approaches me.

"I see you've done yoga before."

"Oh yeah, I try to go whenever I have time."

"I'm Meredith, by the way."

"It's a pleasure! I'm Emily."

I extend my hand and am met with hers. Our handshake is gentle, yet firm at the same time. I'm used to getting a sense of people from their handshakes. The feeling I get from hers is comforting and grounding.

"Do you live here?"

"No, I'm just vacationing. I live in Chicago."

"Chicago is great! I used to live there until recently."
Her voice is nostalgic and a bit sad. I guess she
misses the city. Do I miss it? Good question. I don't
know. Chicago is indeed a great place to live. It's a
pity I have mostly sad memories associated with it
lately.

"Miami has better weather," I joke, to lighten both of
our moods.

"No argument there." She laughs and visibly
relaxes.

"How long have you been teaching yoga?"

"A couple of years already. It all started because I
needed an emotional outlet, and yoga was it for
me. I loved it so much, I built my career and
business around it. If you can't live without it, might
as well live with it to the fullest."

"It's amazing! You're the second person I've met
here over the past few days who's turned a passion
into their life's work." The other, of course, being
Alex and his passion for boats.
"Really? Interesting. I didn't think about it that
way. It's just that back when I started doing yoga
professionally, it seemed the only way to stay sane."
She casts her eyes downward for a second, as

though she regrets saying too much.

"I use it to keep my sanity too. Brings me peace and clarity." I really like her. She has a vibe I relate to so naturally—maybe it's because we both use yoga to cope with our anxiety.

"I completely agree. I feel better after each class, even if I don't practice and just teach." A sad smile stretches over her lips, but doesn't reach her eyes.

"You do an amazing job teaching. I've seen dozens of instructors over the years and let me tell you, even after just one class, you are in my all-time, top-three list." I smile brightly, my words one-hundred-percent true.

"No way!" She laughs heartily.

"For sure! This is not some lame compliment. I really loved it! When is your next practice?"

"Aw, thank you! I'm teaching every day at nine and noon. This two o'clock is usually taught by my partner, Lorrie. I'm just substituting today."

"Perfect, then I'll see you tomorrow in the morning!"

"Great, I'll be looking forward to it."

With a smile, I push the door open and step out into the hot Miami air. The class had a great effect on my mood, making me calmer and more optimistic. I feel I have the strength to face whatever life throws at me next. Maybe I should start all over, here in

Miami, build my business from scratch, do it my way. An unusual wave of positivity washes over me. I am so lucky. I have managed to meet two very different people who inspire me with the way they take control of their lives and do what they love. The thought of Alex makes me miss him more. I wonder why he hasn't called.

My condo is eerie-quiet and empty. I slide all of the curtains and shades open to fill the rooms with a view of the endless ocean. As much as I appreciate this serenity, I need something to distract me from my thoughts of Alex. I put my phone into the speaker dock and turn on my playlist. Some music would be great.

To my surprise, the condo is equipped with a speaker system that plays the music in every room. I sway my hips to the beat, making my way to the bathroom. The sound surrounds me at every turn. I tug at my sweaty yoga outfit and remove it instantly, feeling the cool air on my hot skin. Stepping under the water jets, I let them shoot at me from every direction and massage my tense muscles. Even in the shower, I'm surrounded by the beat of my favorite songs by Maroon5.

After showering and throwing on a swimsuit and cover up, I head downstairs to have lunch at the café by the pool. Hopefully the sun will roll over the buildings to the west and leave the beach in shade. I can't think of a better ending to the day than shell picking.

As I'm munching on my salad, I feel eyes on me

145

again. Looking around, I see not even one familiar face, but the feeling is nagging at me. Dismissing the idea as a case of paranoia, I try to think of something pleasant. Looking at the ocean and waves brings back thoughts of Alex. My heart aches; I miss him too much.

Adrian is at his cabana, as usual. Waving a hello, he takes my towels and spreads them over a recently vacated reclining chair right in front of the water.

I lie down under the umbrella, watching the waves come and go, thinking and rethinking about how I've spent just a few days with Alex, but feel closer to him than I ever did to Matthew.

Alex just accepts me as I am, no improvement necessary.

Matthew, on the contrary, only wants to see the well-polished edition, superficial emotions, and none of the true me. Why hadn't I seen this before?

I must have dozed off for a little, because the next time I open my eyes, the sun is low behind the buildings and the beach is shaded. Chills run through my body as the wind blows harder.

Stretching on the lounge chair, I feel a pleasant ache in my muscles from all the vigorous activity of the past few days. Between Alex and yoga practice I am feeling sore *everywhere*.

The display on my phone shows five p.m., and no calls or messages from Alex. I feel a pang of disappointment, but quickly push it away.

Having nowhere to go and nothing to do is a new feeling for me. I consider my options, and reason that staying by the beach is the easiest one. As the beach service guys start storing away the chairs and umbrellas, I gather my stuff and go for a walk by the water. Surprisingly enough, it's not as cold as I remembered it being the last time I went swimming. I walk along the beach, threading through the shallow waves. In and out, in and out, the ocean is alive, and so comforting.

When I was a little girl, I would collect dozens and dozens of shells, then hide them in my suitcase and secretly take them home to show to my nanny. My mother always made me throw them out, because they were useless and messy, as she put it.

Now, being a grown up, I feel giddy at the thought of yet another freedom I have. Childish, really, but pleasing nonetheless. I'll collect all the shells I like, then put them on display in my condo.

I get so carried away I miss the sunset, and I realize it's late when I can barely make out the shells I'm picking. Feeling slightly disoriented, it takes me a minute to figure out how far I've walked. I'm way past the pier and the tall buildings. I think I made it down to the public beach. Yep, I did. I dread the walk back home, alone in the dark, and contemplate crossing the beach and catching an Uber on Collins.

I start heading away from the water in the direction I think Collins should be. I hope the stretch here is as narrow as it is up north, by the hotel. The sand slowly turns into gravel, and I put my flip-flops on. The trail takes turns surrounded by tall tropical bushes with big, round leaves and occasional palm trees. It's even darker in here, and my heart rate picks up.

Deep breath in, slow exhale, deep breath in, slow exhale. I try not to panic, and to watch the trail for any signs of Collins ahead. Suddenly my world comes to a stop, I can't move, can't breathe, can't scream. Someone grabs me from behind and covers my mouth with a large, rough hand, holding my body hostage with the other one. I'm pushed ahead toward the small shelter building that houses a rest area, vending machines, and bathrooms.

He's dragging me to the men's bathroom. My panic doubles. Graphic images form in my mind. My legs are useless, paralyzed by fear. I sense his huge frame behind me and feel completely helpless. His breath is hot in my ear, growling something. He speaks in a rough whisper, and my fear-fogged mind can barely make out the words.

"You will pay for your defiance."

I'm getting dizzy from the lack of oxygen, his massive hand covering too much of my face. Hopelessness settles in, and I go limp in his hold. He growls deeper as he is burdened with the weight of my sagging body.

Then he collides with something and drops me to the ground with a thump. I open my mouth to gulp oxygen, and feel an immediate rush of adrenalin in my veins. I jump from the ground, only to discover him fighting another guy. I have no idea what's going on, and I don't intend to find out either.

My legs start moving and soon, I'm running full speed toward the lights of Collins, finally visible behind the tall palm trees. The trail doesn't go straight—it veers around, teasing me with its close proximity to the still-inaccessible road ahead. I hear loud steps behind, running faster and approaching me. I run as fast as I can, but it's no good.

Stealing a glance behind me, I see a man just a few steps away now. He is not the same one who grabbed me; he's the other guy, the one who'd gone after my attacker.

"Wait, I'm not going to hurt you," he says, his deep voice right behind me.

I'm in shock and can't stop running, not willing to take a chance and be captured again. In a few steps, he catches up with me and grabs and lifts me off the ground in a clean swipe, dropping to the side of the trail and into the tall grass. He falls on his back, cradling me to his chest. I try to fight him, but he holds me tightly, rocking slightly from side to side.

"Shhh... I'm not going to hurt you. I promise!" His voice is quiet and comforting.

The fight leaves me and I sag against his wide chest. His heartbeat is loud against my ear. I try to catch my breath, feeling tired and powerless. I can't begin to decipher what has just happened. I only hope I'm not making a mistake now. My senses are no longer firing off; I feel safe in his strong arms.

When my breathing becomes steadier, he lifts up from the ground, sitting with me in his lap. I look at his face, dark eyes staring straight at me. There is no menace in them. Only worry and protectiveness. Who is he?

"Are you ok now? Will you try running away if I let you go?"

"I'm ok, I won't run." I couldn't even if I wanted to, I'm too exhausted.

"Did I hurt you when we fell? I tried to stop you but you wouldn't."

"I'm ok. I'm not hurt, just scared as hell. Are you ok? I think I fell right on top of you."

"That was the plan." He smiles now. His face is tough, but the smile is open and friendly. His dark hair is cropped short, thick eyebrows hang low above big dark eyes. There is a vertical scar on his left eyebrow, a thin line cutting across. Strong cheekbones and a face covered in short stubble make him look positively murderous. Until he smiles, that is, and gazes at me with that protective look in his eyes. I feel safe. Crazy, but true.

"Are you done studying me?" He cocks his scarred eyebrow at me.

"I don't bite, I promise."

"I'm sorry. It's still hard to believe what almost happened. And you, you saved me. Thank you! I'm so lucky you happened to be there."

I can't keep eye contact any longer, or I'll melt into a pool of tears. I look down into my trembling hands, clasped together at my lap. A shudder runs through my body and I begin to tremble all over. He hugs me tentatively and whispers calming words in my ear. It takes a few minutes, but he succeeds and I calm down again. Then he wastes no time, lifting from the ground while keeping me in a tight hug. I'm lifted like a feather, and he starts walking with me toward the road.

I protest and beg to be put down, promising to not run and to be able to walk on my own. He relents and soon my feet are on the gravel path, taking shaky steps. Our pace slows down with my tentative steps. My knees are not steady, but I refuse to admit it. I take the arm he offers, and we walk in silence for a few minutes.

"What happened to the guy who attacked me?"

"He's going to think twice before he ever does it again."

"Did you beat him and leave him there? What if he goes mad and attacks another girl? Although I doubt anyone is stupid enough to be as careless as I was."

"First of all, you are not careless, stop with that self-projecting guilt trip. Second, I doubt hurting anyone will be on his agenda for the foreseeable future."

"So, in other words, the guy is lucky to be alive after he met you in person?" I look up at his face but again see no menace. Looking down at me he simply says:

"We all choose our actions and must face the consequences."

As if this was planned. To choose being a criminal or a retaliator.
We're approaching the road, and I realize I never learned my savior's name.

"I'm Emmeline." I extend my small hand, and he wraps it gently in his massive one.

"I'm Victor."

"Nice to meet you, and thank you again! I really have no words to express how grateful I am."

He gently puts his other hand on top of the one that's holding mine.

"There's no need to thank me. Anyone in my place would have done the same. I'm just lucky to have been there at the right time. It's always nice to put scumbags where they belong. I'm just really sorry it all happened to you. Must have scared the living shit out of you."

"It did." I look up straight into his eyes, tilting my head all the way to reach the height of his six and a half feet, no less. It's a challenge, at my five and a half.

"Thank you!"

"You are most welcome. I would do it all over in a heartbeat."

We turn back to walking in silence until we're at the intersection of Collins and the park entrance. I realize I need to call an Uber, but he beats me to it.

"I'll take you to your place. For my peace of mind. Just want to make sure you get there safely."

"Um, ok. Are you sure? I can manage."

"Yes, please don't deny me the peace of mind."

"Thank you, again!" I give him my address and he types it in.

"Two minutes and it'll be here. White Camry."

I look at the road, spotting a white Toyota approaching us. I have no clue how to tell if it's a Camry or not a Camry unless I'm reading the label on the back, so I point to it. Victor laughs.

"This is not a Camry. Good thing I'm still here."

I purse my lips and keep looking at the road until I spot another white car in the distance. I give him a silent look and he nods.

"Now that's our ride."

I wonder to myself, how do guys do this? Then again, they're guys, cars are their toys.

The car stops and we get in. Victor opens the door for me, but sticks his head in for a second to check out the inside. Then I climb in, followed by him. He takes up too much space in the back, and I push myself against the other door to give him room. Poor guy. With his height and build he should be driving something huge, not sitting in the back.

The car starts rolling but soon stops in a traffic jam. There must be an accident ahead of us. All lanes but one are closed.

We're sitting silently, listening to some elevator music the driver has playing in the car.

"You know, I keep thinking about that creep. It's weird, but I don't think it was an accident he was there. I know it sounds crazy, but I think he's been after me for some time. I felt someone watching me all evening."

I figure I shouldn't mention feeling someone watching me ever since I got to Miami. That'll sound outright crazy.

Victor gives me a long look, his eyes telling me he knows what I'm talking about.

"Have you ever felt eyes on you? You know what I mean?" I look at him questioningly, hoping he doesn't think I'm some crazy lunatic wandering deserted trails in the dark looking for trouble.

"I know exactly what you mean." He's quiet again.

"The good news is, regardless of how long he might have followed you, he's gone now and is not likely to be coming back any time soon."

I consider his words, finding some peace in them.

I relax against the door again, peeking around the driver's seat to check the size of the traffic jam ahead. Looks like we're almost there.

"So, do you often save ladies in the middle of deserted beaches?"

Victor's presence and his reassurance of the thug's departure has me feeling better by the minute.

"I'm the knight of the night!" He laughs and his eyes are softer now, less worry in them.

"Just missing some armor," I joke, playing along and looking at his barely-covered form, grey cargo shorts and a tight, dark T-shirt being the only armor to speak of.

"Uh-huh, you just thanked me a few minutes ago,

and now you're picking on my armor?" He makes a funny sad face, and I cannot keep from laughing.

"Summer armor is perfectly fine, Miami-style knight!" I giggle in response.

"You would not believe what I can do in this armor!" He gives me a long meaningful look and then winks.

I'm left debating whether part of the joke was the actual truth. His looks and overall endurance are worthy of a soldier.

I'm debating asking him straight-up if he ever served when the car turns and we approach the lobby of my building. Victor gets out of the car and extends his strong arm to hold me up. I notice he has some tattoos on his forearms that I hadn't spotted before; they're on the back side, running from his elbows down to his wrists. I don't catch what they say.

"I'll take you to your door and leave."

"You really don't have to. I'll be ok."

"I insist. Let me be a true knight and deliver you to your castle." He gives me a small bow of his head, and I just laugh.

"This is not an attempt to come home with you. I swear! It would just make me feel good knowing you're safe inside." He sounds earnest.

"Ok, yes, thank you. I really didn't think you were trying to come home with me..."

I catch myself realizing I really do not get that kind of vibe from him. Protective, yes; flirty, no.

Victor sticks his head back into the vehicle and asks the driver to wait for him for five minutes while he takes the lady upstairs.

We enter the building and I head to the elevators. Victor is close behind me, and in less than a minute we are in front of my door.

"I'm here. Thank you very much for walking with me."

"It was my pleasure. Too bad we had to meet under these circumstances."

"Oh well. I'm so happy you were there. It would have been worse if we hadn't met."

"True."

"Thanks again!"

"Don't mention it. I'll see you around."

"Yeah, see you around."

As I swipe my card to open the door, Victor turns to head back to the elevators. I look at him one last time, and get inside.

Chapter 13

The condo is unsurprisingly crispy-cool and quiet. I rush to close the door, making sure all locks are locked. Being alone is getting to me. My phone goes back to the speaker dock and music fills the space, reaching to the farthest corners. I need to break the silence, or else I'll drive myself nuts listening for every little sound. After tonight's events I'm in no mood to go out for dinner alone, so I order it in.

Swaying my hips to the beat of the music, I make my way to the bathroom, undress, and step into the hot shower. Standing under the scalding water, I try to make sense of what just happened. It was all too bizarre to comprehend.

There I was, in the middle of a beach, at one of the most upscale places in Miami. You would think I should have been safe.

I keep replaying the events in my mind, and the eyes of that creep keep popping up. He reminds me of Matthew, the Matthew only I know, the one who shows up behind closed bedroom doors. Those are the scary, dangerous eyes of a predator. Even though I was never raped, I felt used. He had this way about him that made me feel inadequate. He came, took what he wanted, and left.

My vision blurs and tears sting my eyes. I realize

I'm crying hysterically. Washing my face, I turn the water cold and gasp in shock. Then I turn it back to scalding hot, before turning it off completely. The tears are somewhat gone, washed away and chased by the streams of cold water. I look in the mirror and command myself not to cry.

Even though I'm staying in, I still get dressed in a casual dress. One of my new purchases: a white, jersey cotton dress that hugs me at the top and flows freely from waist down to below my knees. Just cute enough, without being overdressed. I refuse to feel like a victim.

As I'm looking through my shell collection scattered out on the table, I hear a knock and jump.

"Room service!"

I open the door and let the lady roll in a table with my dinner.

She quickly sets everything up on the dining table next to all the shells. I thank her with a few bucks and lock up after she leaves, double-checking all my locks again.

The room fills with the aroma of my dinner, and my stomach rumbles. I didn't realize how hungry I was.

The food is delicious, or maybe I'm just starving, or maybe it's both. Regardless, I'm glad no one is watching me. I'm not eating like the lady my mother insisted I should be. Instead, I'm going at my food. The salad, pasta, and a piece of apple pie are gone in no time. The carb overload, topped with wine, makes me sleepy. I make quick work of putting the dishes outside my door, and go to lie down on the balcony. Grabbing a throw from the couch, I wrap myself in it and get comfortable. The ocean is still, and the waves are practically silent. I look at the moon over the horizon and feel my lids getting heavy.

* * *

I watch her again, just briefly.

Same spot, same delicious body.

She's become my addiction.

I couldn't stay away, even if I tried.

Especially after today.

* * *

I want to dream of Alex, but my thoughts keep taking me to my past. The predatory eyes of the stranger keep showing up and blending with Matthew's eyes. I feel helpless and inadequate—the way Matthew made me feel in bed, as if I was worthless. Nothing I did ever pleased him. He was always criticizing me. There were never any compliments, just complaints about me not being sensual or sensitive, and instead too frigid and stiff. I feel terrified, as I did with him, afraid of doing the wrong thing. My mind is playing games with me, making my whole body go tight, as it did back home with Matthew. The most painful memories—his bitter words, his cold eyes—keep replaying in my mind. The way he would make me feel cheap and used during sex, unceremoniously taking what he wanted.

I'm shivering from the night's cool breeze and can no longer hold back. I jerk up suddenly and realize I'm crying, as I'm choking on my own tears.

At the same time, a pair of strong arms lifts me from the chair, and I freeze in fear. I'm still in my dream; I'm paralyzed, and blinded by my tears.

I try to scream. Someone is holding me tight, saying something in my ear, but I'm in panic and can't make out the words. I have no strength to fight. My limbs go limp, and I hang my head in defeat. I'm losing the battle, and I refuse to open my eyes and look at my attacker.

Right when I think it's all over for me, I'm placed back on the chair. Familiar hands touch my face, and I feel a gentle and very familiar kiss on my forehead. I open my eyes slowly, afraid of what I'd find, and see Alex. His face is stricken with pain. His eyes are glassy, a shade of metallic grey I've never seen before.

"Angel, oh Angel. I'm sorry, I didn't mean to scare you. You were just there, crying, I'm sorry."

He's whispering and lightly rubbing his thumbs over my cheeks, wiping at the tears. Despite his overall state of despair, Alex's nearness has a profound calming effect on me. I suddenly feel safe.

"It's ok, I ... I had a bad dream, it happens, sometimes." I try to focus and look at his face, so close to mine. It's ashen with worry.

"How did you get in? When?" I hate that he saw me in all of my desperate glory, disoriented, scared, crying, fighting him. Oh god, I never meant for him to witness this.

"I called you time and time again but you never answered. I got worried and came by as soon as I could, but you wouldn't open the door." He pauses for a second and looks down, continuing quieter.

"Then I used my resources and got the keys to your place. I knew you were inside, I could hear your music. I was going absolutely crazy with worry because you wouldn't answer the door."

163

He still gently holds my face in his hands. I've never seen him so shaken up.

"And then I walked in, and you were nowhere to be found. I called out your name and ran through the rooms only to find you crying on the balcony. You looked like you were in agony. You looked like you were... hurting..." His voice is almost a whisper.

"I'm sorry, I never meant for you to see me like this. I really wish you didn't. I'm sorry, I should have kept my phone with me, but I left it at the speaker dock. I'm sorry."

"Don't be. Don't apologize." He bends to kiss my forehead again.

"We all have our demons. God knows, I do too. I should have come back earlier. I meant to, but I got tied down with stuff and couldn't leave."

"Come on, get up, lie with me." I tug at his arm, lifting from the chair. I feel freezing, and another shiver runs through my body. I need him, need to feel his warm body pressed to mine, need to feel enveloped in his strong arms, to feel protected, if only from my own dreams.

As we settle back into the chair, Alex senses my need for him and cradles me in his arms, holding me in a bear hug. I relish his closeness.

"Why were you so worried for me?" I'm not sure how much of my nightmare he'd seen, but I'm sure it hadn't been pretty. I really hope it didn't turn him away from me, or worse, make him pity me.

There is a pause. He must be contemplating his answer.

"What are you thinking?" I turn to look in his eyes. I desperately hope there's no pity there. Instead, I see him looking blindly in front of himself, lost in thought.

"Alex?"

His voice is flat, emotionless. He's distancing himself from the memories.

"When I was thirteen, my father was making a name for himself in the business world. He'd been threatened before, but he'd always ignored it. Then, I got kidnapped." Alex sucks in a deep breath and goes on.

"It took a while before I was free again." He is quiet, a small tremor shakes his body, and I hug him tightly.

"While I was kept there, I witnessed things, pretty bad things." His voice starts shaking with emotion, and he falls silent.

I'm stunned, and at a complete loss for words. Never in a million years did I expect him to say something like that. I turn to face him and hug him tighter, trying to shield him from the oncoming memories. I know better than to pity him.

He continues with a renewed sense of strength.

"The things they did to women, those images are imprinted in my mind; they've haunted me for years. When I saw you just now, your face, your cries—there was something terribly wrong there."

He rubs his eyes and shakes his head, as if shaking the memories away. If only he knew how close he'd come to the embarrassing truth of my past.

"I've never shared this story with anyone before. I'm not even completely sure why I'm telling you. It just seems so natural to talk to you. Everything seems so natural with you." His voice is a soft whisper, turning from painful to hopeful.

His grip on me is tighter now, his hot breath on my neck. I revel in his arms and search for strength in his embrace. Now it's my turn to push away the memories. I fall silent, just holding him tight, gathering the energy to talk.

"I was alone at the beach today and went much farther south than I usually do. It had gotten dark before I realized it. This weird guy came at me from out of nowhere; he looked crazy and wanted to hurt me. I'm almost certain he *would have* hurt me, were it not for a stranger who intervened."

I feel Alex tighten his grip, and I can barely breathe. He sucks in a breath, but does not dare interrupting me.

I stop and try to inhale and exhale deeply, to avoid another meltdown. I have to be strong.

Then I feel an urgent need to share a little of my story with Alex, to let him in like he'd done for me. For once in my life, I feel capable of facing my demons—just not all at once. I'll share a little bit at a time, watching for the effect it has on Alex. This side of my life, the one no one knows about, is eating away at me, and I need to open up, to let go of the past and look into the future. The future, where there are no pretenses, no shame, no secrets, just bare me. I take another deep inhale and go on.

"I feel the same way you do. I don't want to pretend with you. My whole life I've been living up to someone else's standards, and what's worse, pretending I liked it. My trip to Miami is not coincidental, not just a beach vacation for the sake of getting a nice tan. I came here with a mission to sort my life, find my true self, decide what to do next. I can't just pretend to be happy anymore. I thought I had it all, the professional and personal life, but it's falling apart. The personal part came down first, now I'm about to crash the professional part too."

Alex is quiet, just holding me, letting me talk while he listens. His tight hold on my body gives me the strength and support I need to continue talking. This is the first time I'm saying these things out loud, and it makes everything more real. I have no idea if this will scare him off, if I'll be left alone. If that's what's meant to happen, then so be it. I have to get this off my chest. I no longer want to pretend or avoid. If there's ever going to be anything between us, it has to be built on the complete and utter truth and trust.

"On the outside, I have it all. A set of successful parents to look up to, a degree from a prestigious university, blooming career growth, and a fiancée who shares my business ideas."

Alex tenses as I mention the fiancée, but he doesn't let go of me; he just reinforces his grip. I draw strength from his hold and the overall sense of safety he seems to exude. Turning to look into his eyes, I search them for signs of disapproval or alienation, but neither is there. His eyes are warm and filled with such care, it's hard to believe we've only known each other for less than a week.

Feeling a renewed charge of self-confidence, I break eye contact, looking out at the ocean instead, and continue.

"In reality, however, things are nowhere near as peachy. I have virtually no relationship with my parents, except for business interactions and social functions when we pretend to be a happy family. I have lived a pretend life for a long time, but I've gotten used it, really. What threw me off balance was my fiancée. He was my parents' protégé. They were the ones who set me up with him, and I assumed he was a decent person. I found out he hasn't been faithful. I've been getting hints from our friends, but I always refused to believe this could be happening. Now, too many things are falling into place. I'm not sure how long he's been doing it. I was aware our relationship wasn't perfect; we lacked intimate feelings for each other. But that was just the final nail in the coffin. I could justify his coldness, rationalize it being due to his age, explain the lack of feelings as maybe my own coldness. I cannot live with a deceitful person. I broke up with him before coming here."

Breaking my stare away from the ocean, I look back at Alex. His face is serious and his jaw is clenched. He's fighting an internal battle of some kind. I wish I'd never said anything. It looks like I'm losing the only person who seems to care about me, just me. On second thought, he cares for the girl he wants to see, not the girl I've revealed myself to be. Hurt spreads through my chest and rises up to choke my throat. I look away, focusing on the ocean to suppress the tears. Wave after wave, it hits the beach, forming silvery-white foam. Then, the magic disappears; the white foam slowly dissipates. Until another wave hits the shore, forming the pearly bubbles that themselves will soon be swallowed up by the dark waters. It makes me think of meeting Alex. The magic was there from the moment we met, but it's starting to disappear, swallowed by the darkness and ugliness of reality. How ironic.

"Angel, look at me." Alex's hand snakes around my neck and his finger graze my chin. I hesitate for a moment before turning my face to him. The irony of the whole situation is sitting heavy in my chest, not letting me take a deep breath.

"I know I looked upset, but I wasn't upset with you, I was mad at the things you had to go through." He kisses my forehead, and the heaviness feels a little lighter. I try to relax in his arms.

"I care for you, like I haven't cared for anyone in a very long time." His lips are on my forehead, kissing gently, trying to kiss away the worry that must be showing there again. I can't hide from him. And surprisingly enough, for the first time ever, I don't want to. Looking in his eyes I say:

"I care for you too. When I'm with you I feel safe."

"I will do everything in my power to keep you safe. I promise!" Alex's eyes are on fire, full of emotion, making my heart skip a beat. There is so much emphasis in his words, so much meaning he's trying to convey. I realize no one ever said anything like that to me before. Running my hands along his jawline I whisper:

"Make love to me." My lips touch his, and he opens his mouth to let our tongues dance together.

I wrap my arms around Alex's neck and broad shoulders, while he slides his arms under my butt and lifts off the chair. Stepping inside, he goes straight to the dining room.

My dress goes first, then his shirt, both flying over our heads. I am standing in front of him in my nude lacy underwater, while he is bare chested with low-hanging jeans. I turn my head to the mirrored wall and our gazes meet. We're both panting, chests rising and falling, but in this moment, I see us together, half-naked, overflowing with desire, and I have never seen anything more beautiful.

He comes behind me, runs his palms along my flat stomach, kissing my neck, all the while keeping eye contact in the mirror. I look at how perfectly we fit together, like yin and yang. My lightly tanned skin against his darker flesh, his muscular frame bending over my smaller, feminine one.

Alex opens my bra clasp in the front and cups my breasts in his large hands. He gently kneads on them, cupping their weight and pushing them together as his thumbs get under the lace of my bra and find my nipples. He strokes the tender peaks softly, and I feel moisture building between my legs. My nipples get hard and I pant and writhe my body against his. My butt finds his bulging erection and I rub against it. He groans and pushes his leg between mine. His hands lose their hold on my bra and it falls down my arms and onto the floor revealing my breasts, heavy with desire, their weight no longer supported. My beaded nipples are hard and pink against the white triangles the swimming suit left around them.

Alex's hands glide along my hips, up my waist, brushing lightly over my ribs and finally getting back to the underside of my breasts, his touch sending jolts of electricity through my body. My head falls back on his shoulder.

"Look at me!" His voice is raspy, but the tone is

demanding. My head flies up and our eyes meet in the mirror. The worry in his eyes is gone, instead replaced by heat and desire. His eyes are burning into me, demanding constant contact with mine.

Strong hands cup my breasts and start rolling my nipples, and I almost close my eyes again. A pinch on one nipple, border lining on painful, has my attention back on Alex's eyes. My mouth is slightly open, I lick my lips and struggle to keep in place. My arms are at my sides and I raise them to go around his neck and pull him closer to me. I arch my back reaching for him, riding his thigh, creating a much-needed pressure on my clit and pushing my breasts into his hands in offering. He chuckles softly and keeps rolling my nipples between his thumbs and forefinger, applying more pressure as he goes. He learned my hot spot pretty quickly.

I try to wiggle out and turn to face him, but he has a strong hold on me, keeping eye contact all the while. I'm panting and moaning. Then his right hand lets go of my nipple and breast and moves lower, to my ribs, waist, running a circle around my belly button, only to resume on its path lower and lower until it reaches the perfectly waxed and bare skin of my bikini line. His foot pushes slightly against mine to part my legs a little wider. Once I oblige, his fingers move lower and cup my sex. I take a sharp breath in, unable to stand still, and squirm against his body.

"Don't move!" He whispers in my ear.

I oblige again, surprised at how naturally it comes to

me. As I submit to his will, I feel desired and worshipped.

His hand is still cupping my sex through the lace of the underwear. Feather-light touches are mixed with more intense ones. The sequence is unpredictable and totally driving me crazy. The lace is soaking wet when it is pushed to the side, and his fingers open my folds, soaked with moisture from my arousal. With no delay, he finds my tight bud and settles on running gentle, mind-blowing circles over it. I moan aloud, a sound so carnal and unfamiliar I almost doubt it comes from me.

I'm getting close, every ounce of my body feels alive. Then, when I'm ready to lose it, he removes his hand completely. I whimper at the loss and beg him to continue. He grabs a chair with one hand and drags it closer to us.

"Put your foot on the cushion and open your hips." His eyes are on me. I blush and try to protest.

"Do it, don't think. I want you to see how beautiful you are when you come." I can't argue—my body is still buzzing with an anticipated orgasm, and his words make me even more aroused.

I reluctantly put my foot up on that chair, and he opens my knee to the side, revealing my sex in the mirror in all its glistening glory. I can't pull my eyes away from it. This is simple, yet so sexy. This is my body, but I feel as if I'm discovering it for the first time.

His takes my arm in his and moves us down to my pelvis. I'm self-conscious and can't concentrate, my fingers feeling foreign to me. I've never pleasured myself in front of anyone. He kisses my shoulder, running a trail of kisses up my neck and grazing his teeth over my jawline.

"Relax, just do what feels good." His words are a faint whisper in my ear.
I drop my head back over his shoulder and relax against him. My eyes close on their own accord and I try to run my fingers over my swollen lips. The touch makes me shiver. Then I feel his fingers pushing inside of me. I gasp and push against him, the sensation overwhelming.

"Open your eyes!" His voice is commanding. My head flies up again and our eyes meet in the mirror.

"Look at yourself, look how beautiful you are!"

I look over my body, from my eyes filled with lust, to my wet lips, to my heavy breasts with peaked, hard nipples. His body is wrapping mine, strong shoulders and arms around mine, hugging my waist, his leg next to mine on the chair to allow me something to lean on. Our hands interlaced on my sex, mine rubbing, his plunging in and out. The image burns itself into my memory. This is the sexiest thing I've ever done. I'm mesmerized by our reflection. The orgasm is approaching with a renewed force, wave after wave coursing through my body, coiling in my core. I'm climbing the mountain of pleasure, ready to be pushed over the top. I look him straight in the eye.

"I'm close, oh Alex, don't stop now. More, more.....oh Alex."

As his name falls off my lips, he plunges inside of me one last time and I'm done. The orgasm rips through my body with such force that my knee buckles. I'm caught by his strong arm and lean back against his chest, my core clenching around his fingers as he lets me ride the waves of pleasure. I struggle to keep my eyes focused, and as the last aftershocks leave my body, my eyes close and my head falls back on his shoulder.

He moves just a bit and is sitting on the chair in front of the mirror. I'm lowered onto his lap and gently guided to push his rigid cock inside of me. I gasp at feeling his length entering me. My eyes fly open. He's holding me up, not letting me swallow him whole. Once our eyes meet, he loosens his hold and I lower myself a little more. The sheer size and width of him makes me hot all over again, and I watch, fascinated, as our bodies meld into each other. I descend until he's buried deep inside of me. Then I push even deeper to feel him reach the farthest corners of my core and squeeze my muscles. Alex exhales a rough breath, holding me in place as he gathers his strength.

"You are so perfect and tight around me. God, you are beautiful."

I see our reflection in the mirror and couldn't agree

with him more. We do look perfect together, as if meant for each other.

I feel him twitch inside of me, and that's my cue. I start moving up, watching his cock leave my body, stopping just barely at the edge before I'd lose him completely, then I plunge forcefully back down, swallowing all of him. He groans and tightens his grip on me. I lift again and watch, hypnotized, the point where our bodies are joined. He guides my moves, slowly up and down, creating the perfect friction to prolong both of our pleasure. I feel him growing thicker and harder, realizing he's close. His hand moves to tease my clit. He knows just the right touch to push my body over the edge. Our eyes are locked in the mirror, fighting to stay open as we both focus on the impeding peak of our pleasure. My insides are coiled and I begin shaking, unable to control it any longer.

"Come with me, now!"

I've never been able to come on the spot, but his skillful fingers and words are my undoing. I close my eyes, if only for a moment, my whole body shaking, and clench tightly around him. A loud groan escapes his lips as he comes hard and fills me, pushing himself deeper inside.

I watch his face and never ever want to miss the view of Alex coming apart. Knowing I did this to him, to this beautiful, strong man who seems flawless and impenetrable on the outside, gives me the strength and self-confidence I've been missing all these years. For the first time, I see myself fully revealed, and I see the effect I can have on a man. The feeling is euphoric. My head is still spinning with images of us in the mirror.

As we both come down from our high, I feel boneless. I want real eye contact, without the mirror, so I turn to kiss his lips. I hold his face in my hands, brushing my lips gently over his, our noses nuzzling, eyes locked.

"Thank you." This is all I can say, but Alex understands the simple phrase is loaded with meaning. He gets me somehow. He knew I needed this, to be reassured of my beauty and confidence. I wish I could see through him as well. He remains a mystery to me. I'm slowly trying to peel away layers of his outer shell. Catching unguarded looks, reading his eyes, gauging emotions. It still feels like scraping at the surface.

He cradles me in his lap. My hands wrap around his neck and I kiss him gently and possessively all at once. I have no claim on him, but my kiss tells him I want him all to myself.

He lifts up effortlessly from the chair and takes us both into the shower. I barely have the strength to stand on my own. In minutes, we're both clean and back in my bedroom. He puts me on the bed and pulls the sheet over me. I'm not sure if he was planning to leave or stay, but I can't let him go now. I need him, I want him next to me.

"Would you stay the night?"

I look up in his eyes, not knowing what awaits me there. He is tearing down my walls one by one, getting closer to my heart. I never planned on having any feelings, but I can't help what's happening. I need his closeness; I need his intimacy. After what we've done, I need to seal the memories with his touch. Being alone right now will make me doubt all my actions. I have to reassure myself I'm not falling into a rabbit's hole I won't be able to climb back out of.

I must have a whole mix of emotions on my face again. Looking in his eyes, I see relief and concern. He kisses my forehead lightly.

"I thought you'd never ask."

Just like that, no more words are needed. He climbs into bed next to me, settling down on my pillow. I find a comfortable spot in the nook of his arm and press my body against his, tangling our legs. His hand follows slow circles around my back, while the other is holding the arm that was just hugging his chest. He kisses my knuckles gently and whispers.

"Good night, Angel."

"Good night."

I am vividly aware of every inch of our naked bodies touching, but the sensation is so comforting I feel my lids growing heavy as sleep takes me. I want to fight it, to enjoy his touch a while longer, to remember every moment, but soon I'm deep asleep, our breathing in sync, our chests rising and falling together as one.

Chapter 14

I am awakened by my phone, a loud ring that echoes through the entire condo. The damn thing is still plugged into the sound system. I jerk up from the bed and take in my surroundings. The bed is empty, sans me in it. Alex is gone. I check the time: nine thirty. That's way past my normal waking hour. I guess the events of last night completely wore me out. Knowing from our runs together that Alex is a morning bird, I'm not too surprised he's gone.

The familiar ping of voicemail rings through the air, breaking the silence. Reluctantly, I get up from the bed and go to retrieve my phone. I go around naked, not stopping to put anything on and completely unbothered by it. Talk about what one therapeutic sex session can do for my ego...

The missed call is from my father. The presence of a voicemail makes me anxious. What could have possibly happened that he would be calling me at half past eight, their time? I turn it on and listen, my heart beating at an erratic pace. I hate that he makes me feel so nervous.

"Hello, Emily. I need you back in Chicago immediately. There is a situation that needs to be addressed without any delays. Kelly has the next available flight booked for you. Call her and get the details. I'll see you later today."

Just like that, he has me flying to Chicago on a moment's notice. So like him. No consideration for my plans. The frustration is building inside of me like a summer storm. How dare he? What could be so important?

I dial my assistant's number and get the flight info. While talking to her, I ask if she knows what happened, but she has no clue. Things are as planned, nothing out of the ordinary. No loose ends on any of my deals. Now I am even more confused and mad.

Packing just a few essentials, I head to the airport. There's no way I'm cutting my time in Miami short. I call Kelly back and tell her to book me on the last flight out of Chicago today. Then I shoot a quick text to the number Alex left the other day, letting him know I have to tend to business in Chicago, and that I'd be gone for the day.

Despite wanting to drive my rental convertible to the airport, I decide against it. I'll be flying in at an ungodly hour, exhausted, so best to avoid driving. Besides, if I get stuck in Chicago longer, the airport parking bill will not be pretty. So, Uber it is.

I-95 is barely moving, an accident ahead blocking several lanes. I check my watch every few minutes, anxiety building higher each time. I can't be late. Kelly booked me to fly out of Miami, the bigger of the two local airports and a nightmare to get to. Luckily, I should be flying into Fort Lauderdale. It's closer and easier to get in and out of.

I barely make it on time for the flight, thankful I have no luggage to check in. As I step onboard, a different kind of anxiety sets in. Damn planes, I hate flying. I take a seat by the window and try to relax and steady my breathing. The hardest part, takeoff, is still ahead. I should start drinking something strong, or taking tranquilizer pills. But the control freak in me cannot deal with a clouded mind. Especially when I'm on my way to meet with my father. Never a pleasant event. God knows I've tried to please him, to look past all the criticism I've heard my whole life. I have tried in vain.

Our interactions have been curtailed to the bare minimum—modern methods of communication allow me to keep him keep him up-to-date on business deals while avoiding any real, personal contact. My life has been gradually getting easier. I can even pretend at times he's not overshadowing every step I'm taking and every decision I am making. No matter how successful my track record is, my deeds are never enough, and I'm never fully trusted. Oh well, there's nothing I can do. I'm just happy to be building business relationships under my own name and creating a positive and trustworthy image with my clients and associates.

What bugs me though is, what could have possibly happened that he requested I fly back right away? I think and rethink the latest deals, looking for a flaw, loose end, or leak of information. All in vain. I know how I work, so it must be something else. But what? That's a good question.

My thoughts are interrupted by the captain's announcements. We're on time and will be lifting off in minutes. I assume my iron hold on the armrests, close my eyes, and concentrate fully on breathing evenly. Inhale through my nose—one, two; exhale through my mouth—three, four. One, two, three, four. One, two, three, four. I'm pushed into the seat as the Boeing accelerates and we lift off. One, two, three, four. One, two, three, four. Finally, the plane reaches a higher altitude and I open my eyes to an endless horizon of blue skies and snow-white clouds. The sun is bright and blinding. Despite its fiery glare, I can't keep my eyes away. At some point my eyes become clouded with tears from the intensity of the light outside, but my mind is calmer, the serenity of the view working its wonders as usual.

I give up, lower my lids, and relax back against the seat. My mind wanders to thoughts of Alex. His blue eyes and crooked half-smile when he's teasing me, making me relax in his presence. Glazed-over darkened eyes and partially parted lips when he's aroused, holding me in his strong, skillful hands, taking his time to unravel my insecurities and help me overcome them. He reads my emotions like no one has ever been able to. We know so little about each other, yet have shared extremely intimate moments together. I am drawn to him. It's like a magnetic pool. Yet, I do not feel him infringing on my independence. I want his nearness, yet I'm afraid to lose myself again. I need to become stronger, rather than dependent on another relationship, and what's incredible is, I think Alex senses that. He's been trying to empower me. Give me more confidence. I miss him terribly and wonder what he would have to say about this whole mess, with crazy flights back and forth. I dread the moment I'll be meeting my father. My gut is telling me something big is about to happen. The scared girl in me is trying to break loose. Instead of fear, I realize I feel exasperated.

By the time I get to the office it's past five. Everyone has left, the lights are dimmed all over the floor—just my father's office is lit up. I head right in, stopping briefly to knock on the door. He answers immediately, and I walk in.

He is at his monstrosity of a desk, intended to instill respect and fear at the mere sight of him. I ignore it completely and step right up to him.

"Good evening!" He does not even dignify me with a look, keeping his head down, studying a thick binder of documents.

"You've asked to see me. What's the urgency?"

I make an effort to keep my voice leveled and avoid riling him on. His irritation is palpable in the air, but I refuse to be affected. Still not looking up at me, he tosses a yellow manila envelope in my direction. With no other words or gestures from him, I take hold of it. What's inside? I'm anxious to know, but I won't show it. Instead, I take my time settling down in one of the guest chairs on my side of the table. Once I'm comfortable, I slowly open the envelope and let its contents slide out onto the spotless surface of his polished, redwood table.

The air leaves my lungs and I visibly cave in. The table is littered with glossy images of me in Miami with none other than Alex. We are laughing, kissing, holding hands, getting out of the water, relaxing on the beach. It seems like every minute of our time together in public has been documented. I am stunned and speechless. Then I remember feeling eyes on me all the time and realize I wasn't paranoid, I really *was* being watched. All my resolve is gone, my head spinning with questions. Why? Who? What now?

This is the time my father chooses to raise his eyes and give me the filthiest look he can muster. I think I might have shrunk under his glare. His voice comes as a thunderstorm.

"Care to explain what this is? Did you forget who you are? Did you forget your status in the family and in this company?"

I gather my wits and can't think of anything other than to ask why.

"Why were you spying on me? How dare you?"

"Don't you dare question me!" His eyes are blazing with anger, lips pressed in a thin, straight line. I don't recall ever seeing him this mad.

"I got these from an anonymous source this morning. Along with a note." I lower my gaze back to the table in search of something other than photos of me and Alex. The images are spread around, and

I spread them out more in search of the note. It is there, white paper, small print in the middle stating simply: *Fix this before it becomes public*. I repeat it in my mind, trying to decipher what they mean.

"I'm assuming Matthew has not been enlightened as to your latest escapades. If you're smart, you will keep your family and your reputation intact."

I lift my eyes from the note to look at my father. He has no idea what is going on. Not a clue as to why I went to Miami, or what's going on between me and Matthew. I take a deep breath and brace myself for the reaction I may get once I share my private life with him.

"I left Matthew. Before I went to Miami. He has not been faithful to me and I can't live with that. I have no pictures to show you, but it's true. Besides, I now realize how empty and unhappy I've been these past years. So, there really is nothing to fix." I finish my monologue and look my father straight in the eye. His face contorts with disgust. He puts his elbows on the table and towers his hands up, connecting the very tips of his fingers one to one, in perfect symmetry. His eyes narrow to further show his displeasure with me.

"I want to hear none of that nonsense. You have not been faithful yourself, and what's worse, with the first stranger you met. So now you're even. Fix this, or you will lose everything. I will not tolerate this in my family, or my company. Your choice. Think wisely, and set your priorities straight. And take this filth out of my sight."

I am floored by his reaction. I didn't expect caring, fatherly concern, but this is outrageous. He cares for no one and nothing but himself and his company. My life, happiness, future do not matter to him, not one bit.

With shaky hands, I gather all the images and slide them back into the envelope, along with the threatening note. I get up and head to the door. There's nothing for me to say. It'll fall on deaf ears anyway. His voice booms from behind my back.

"Two days, Emily! I will see you back here on Friday, and we'll take it from there."

A tremor runs through my body and I make a hasty retreat. I can't stay in his presence, breathe the same air any longer. I'm suffocating, both figuratively and literally. Tears are burning the backs of my eyes and a lump forms in my throat. I will not cry here, with the cameras covering every corner of this damn office. I will not grant my father the pleasure of seeing me in tears. My head is up, back straight, pace even as I pass through the hallways of the massive office and head closer to the front door.

I push the heavy double doors open and quickly descend the front steps, turning right and disappearing around the corner, away from the ever-watchful eye of the security cameras. Only once I'm outside the range do I let out a loud gasp and take a few ragged breaths. I was barely breathing, and I can't get enough oxygen. The tears roll down my cheeks, and I feel the freezing wind burning my wet skin. I wipe at my cheeks and shiver in the cold. The weather changed drastically while I was inside. The sun has set completely, and a chill took over the city with the help of the infamous Chicago wind. November in its full glory. Thankfully it's not raining, or even worse, snowing.

I'm still clutching the envelope in my hands, my fingers freezing in the wind. I tuck it in my bag and call a ride back to the airport. I don't intend to stay in this city a minute longer.

On the way to the airport, I call the airline to see if I can switch to an earlier flight. They offer standby on a flight set to leave in just over an hour. If I can make it to the airport fast enough, I still have a chance to be in Miami around midnight.

I make it to the airport, through security, and to the gate right on time. The poor soul who got stuck somewhere amid the crazy Chicago construction and traffic-ridden streets has afforded me the opportunity for a quick retreat back to the warm paradise of Miami.

As I get onboard and settle in, my anxiety comes back, but with noticeably less intensity. I remember my last flight to Miami, and realize it wasn't too bad either. My subconscious must be keeping the anxiety at bay, knowing that better things are ahead.

As the plane accelerates and takes off, I count my breaths. One, two, three, four, one, two, three, four … until we reach altitude. This time there is no serene view to calm my nerves. I am exhausted, mentally and physically. For once, I break my own rules and order a glass of cheap white wine—something to take the edge off. As I'm sipping the cold, sour liquid, I take out the yellow envelope and slowly drag out the photos. My eyes are met by Alex's crooked smile as he looks at my face in the picture. We are so locked in the moment, so completely oblivious to our surroundings that the freak following us could have snapped a picture right in front of our faces and we wouldn't have noticed. I flip through a couple more pictures and every time, I'm met with Alex's eyes, eyes that are completely enthralled by me. That look can't be faked. It is a pure thing. No pretenses. I study every picture, looking at myself and Alex, analyzing us, our body language, eye contact, smiles, postures. I come to the conclusion we are equally captivated by each other. There is something there, a spark that burns brighter with every more recent picture. The images show simple playfulness slowly evolving into fondness, tenderness, affection... love? Can that really be? Am I in love with Alex? Do I know him well enough to be in love? What about him? Isn't it too early? Then again, what about love at first sight? I put these thoughts aside. One step at a time.

What I do realize for certain is that we have something special. Something worth exploring, worth giving a chance to grow bigger, more beautiful. My father and his ultimatums can go to hell. I'm never going back to Matthew. I wish I'd had this resolve when I was in his office today; it would have saved me a trip on Friday. Anyway, I'll fly to Chicago again and end this discussion once and for all. We'll cross the t's and dot the i's. I'm suspecting I will leave the meeting a free, unburdened woman, with no home or job. But isn't that what I wanted all along? Whoever decided to follow me had done me a favor, really...

As I down the rest of my wine, I feel warm and buzzed. I realize I haven't eaten all day.

The descent is smooth, or so it seems, with wine flowing in my blood. I step out of the plane and move unsteadily toward the exit signs. Good job Emmeline! You're tipsy after a single glass of wine. Lightweight!
I'm smiling to myself, my mood drastically better after the flight and setting foot on Floridian soil. I request a ride home and exit the terminal gates. Such a blessing to travel without luggage.

As promised, a silver Volvo shows up in minutes. I climb in and relax against soft leather seats that still smell new. Such a difference from the yellow cabs. The driver is a quiet, older gentleman, and I appreciate the silence.

We arrive at the building I've been calling home for almost a week in less than half an hour. I'm still a little tipsy and totally beat. It's been a long day.

Upstairs, I open the door with my card, finding the place exactly as I left it in the morning. I'm hungry but have no energy to eat. I drop my bag in the closet, grab a newly purchased lacy night gown and head straight to the shower. Five minutes later my face meets the pillows. I can still smell a hint of Alex on my sheets. Nuzzling my face into them, I inhale deeply. His scent invades me and I blissfully fall asleep.

Chapter 15

I dream of Alex, his gentle hands, soft lips, blue eyes, half-smile. The pictures I was looking at on the plane mix with real memories of the times when they were taken. The walk down memory lane is filled with such utter happiness I think I even smile in my sleep, wrapped in sheets that have Alex's unmistakable scent all over them.

I am at the beach, picking shells, finding myself in the dark, looking for my way home. It's too dark, and I lose my sense of direction, lose the trail I was following. It's too dark, even the moon is gone. Panic settles over me, and my breathing becomes erratic. I start running ahead, but there's nothing, nowhere to go. I strain my eyes to try and see the streetlights, or the moon, or anything at all. Suddenly, I'm face-to-face with my attacker, his eyes raging with hatred, his hot breath on my face. I'm numb, frozen by fear. I can't break eye contact with him. Those eyes—predatory, familiar eyes. Are they my father's? As I focus, I realize they belong to Matthew. They're filled with the same contempt and disgust my father's were.

"Now be a good little girl and show me how you love me."

I'm still paralyzed by fear when he orders sharply, "Get on your knees! Now!"

I hear the sound of a zipper opening; he must be working his fly. Tears flow down my face, I'm shaking vigorously in refusal, still not able to speak.

"Get on your knees and suck my dick, now! Show me what I've taught you."

His heavy hands push down on my shoulders, and I can't withstand the weight. I'm pushed down, lower, until I'm eye-level with his waist, on my knees, crying and shaking my head no. He grabs the back of my head as he works to release himself from the confines of his trousers. I push back, straining to scream. Silence. His hand pushes down the underwear and finally, it comes out: a loud, hysterical, soul-tearing scream that wakes me up.

I gasp in the air, still feeling hands pulling me. My body thrashes, and I scream again and again. A weight is settled over my body. I need to break free. I cry and jerk violently, energy leaving me, defeat all too close and familiar.

"It's a dream, just a bad dream, wake up Angel." Gentle hands hold my head, soft lips sprinkle feathery kisses over my tear-streaked cheeks, and a familiar voice whispers softly in my ear.
I stop fighting his hold, peel my eyes open, and attempt to focus on his pain-stricken face. Alex is here, rescuing me from my nightmares, yet again.

He must see the change in my expression, and his hold on me loosens, the weight of his body lifted from mine. I hug his back and push him back onto me. I need to feel his weight, to keep our bodies in contact. It chases the nightmare away. I hold onto him tight, breathing him in, unable to say anything, feeling so ashamed he saw me having a nightmare again.

Alex is quiet, letting me calm down from my hysterical state. As if sensing I need the silence, he says nothing. He just holds me. His face is tucked in the crook of my neck. He is breathing into my skin, suckling lightly at the pulsating vein at my throat. My hands start moving on their own accord, running slow circles over his back, pulling at his T-shirt and sliding under it to get to his skin.

Lifting up just barely, Alex gives me enough room to pull his T-shirt over his head, his hot, naked body settling right back into place.

I still feel disturbed by my dream. I need to erase those images from my mind, replace them with something solid, emotionally strong, pleasant. I act on instinct. I shift under Alex's steel-hard body and he lifts up slightly, giving me room to breathe. I push him off me and climb on top of him. We switch places, so now I lay on top. His hands slide slowly from my shoulders down to my butt, circling the round globes and going back up on their journey to my neck.

I nuzzle into Alex's neck and cover it with wet kisses, running my tongue over his skin. He inhales deeply, and I feel the pace of his heartbeat quicken. My lips begin a slow trip down the familiar, chiseled body, paying attention to every crevice and committing it to memory. I move painfully slowly down his torso, on my mission to get lower and lower until I'm finally at the threshold of his underwear. Alex's cock is barely restrained by the soft material. I run my hand over it, feeling the thick, ridged surface.

Alex exhales a shaky breath, taking a few more ragged ones. He is affected. In fact, he can barely contain himself. Giving me all the power is pushing him to the limit. Once again, I wonder how he knows I need this so desperately.

I pull his boxers down, effectively removing all restraints from his raging erection. Once freed, his cock is up in all of its beautiful glory. I take it in my hand and push down to reveal the glistening head. Alex grunts, and I continue my assault on his flesh. Sliding down between his knees, I wrap two hands around his length and start working him up and down. He grunts and tries to push away my hands.

"Easy there, Angel."

I smile devilishly and lower my lips to his swollen head. I don't take it all in, just kissing the tip and running my tongue around the mushroom top. He pushes his arms into the pillow and I see his muscle bulging. I blow some air on his wet head, and he bucks his hips up to reach my lips. I pull away, just out of reach.

Having mercy on him, I lower my lips and take his head into my mouth. A loud, animalistic sound comes out, and I marvel at the effect I have on him.

My hands work his length while my mouth is sucking on his head. Then I take his cock in, pushing his head all the way into my throat. He's so huge I have to fight tears gathering in my eyes.

I take his balls in my palm and knead them lightly. Finding the perfect sensitive spot under his scrotum, I run one finger along it, back and forth. That does it. Alex's cock becomes rock hard in my mouth, and I know he's so close. I apply more pressure with both my mouth and my fingers.

"Oh Angel, Emmeline, my Eline!"

His hips buck up and push harder into my mouth as he comes violently, hot liquid running down my throat, pump after pump, relieving himself. His hips jerk up each time. I take every last drop of his juice and let go when he is completely exhausted and has nothing left.

I lift my head to see him splayed on the bed, eyes rolled back, limbs powerless. I smile at what I've done to him.

Crawling up his body, I straddle him once again and kiss his lips. He kisses me lazily, as if trying to find strength within himself.

"Thank you for letting me do this. I really needed it," I whisper in his ear, settling on top of him.

My fingertips trace lines along his jawline and neck, going up into his wavy hair. Long lashes cover half-open eyes, and his smile calls the Cheshire Cat to mind.

"Wow, this was unreal."

That's all the confirmation I need. I'm at peace. My eyelids are heavy and I close them knowing I am in strong hands, safe and protected.
Sleep takes me in minutes. As I drift off, I hear Alex's breathing evening out, sleep taking him right along with me.

Chapter 16

I wake up with a start, cold and shaking. The room is dark. The blanket is bunched up next to me in an otherwise empty bed. Reluctantly, I get up to search for Alex. My feet meet the icy cold, marble-tiled floor and another shiver runs through my body. I hope he just couldn't sleep and needed some water. Thinking he might have left me in the middle of the night is just painful. The question is nagging in the back of mind. What if it was too much? The nightmares are a repulsive beast.

I move through the condo without turning on the lights. The glow filtering in from the building across provides enough illumination. The bathroom is empty, as are the kitchen and living room. I feel a pang of disappointment stabbing at my heart. As I'm turning back to the bedroom, I see Alex's silhouette on the balcony, leaning over the rails, clutching his head with both hands. He looks crushed, like he's holding the weight of the world on his shoulders. I hate to be responsible for this. Last time, my nightmare stirred up some nasty old memories in him. Is he in that place again? Reliving the terror of being kidnapped?

My feet quickly eat up the distance to the sliding door. My arms extend to open it and freeze midair, unsure what to do next. I hesitate before stepping out to face him. Standing there in the dark living room, I'm watching this beautiful man and wondering if he would ever want me wholly for who I am, no pretenses, no lies, no omissions. Do we have a chance at completing each other? Or am I his weak link, an unpleasant reminder of the horrible past?

As if sensing my presence, Alex lifts up and turns around. Our eyes meet, and he steps forward the same time I do. With one swift motion, the glass door slides open and I step into his strong embrace.

I inhale his unique scent, gaining strength from his presence.

"You ok?" I look up at him as he hugs me tighter, breathing in my hair, his face muscles relaxing.

"Yeah, just couldn't sleep. Did I wake you?" He's looking down at my face, running a quick scan for signs of another nightmare. Finding none of that he relaxes a bit more, pushing me into his chest. I mumble a reply, barely audible.

"You didn't, I just woke up so cold and alone in the bed. I thought you left."
He replies instantly, lifting up my face. "I would never do that. Not after last night." He doesn't finish, and I know he means my vulnerability after another terrible dream.

My eyes are trained on his, gauging his reaction, looking for proof I'm right.

"I don't know. Maybe it's too much. I hate stirring up old memories in you. I hope it doesn't scare you off. If that happens though, then so be it. I want no more lies in my life, no more pretenses."

"I'm not leaving." His voice is no longer a whisper; it exudes confidence now. His blue eyes convey his resolve. There's not a shadow of a doubt in them.

As if needing to test him further, I start talking, before I can stop myself.
I'm determined to reveal things, some of which I've never said out loud, even to myself.

"What you saw back there, it was a rare but recurring dream. It takes twists, mixes with the reality of the days behind, but the essence is always the same."

He's quiet, listening carefully, eyes on me. I backtrack to explain everything from the beginning.

"This time it mixed in with the incident I had the other day on the beach. The eyes of the attacker, they were the eyes of a predator. I know the look too well. I've lived with it for years. Matthew has eyes like that when we… when he…" I trail off, unable to finish. Until this point Alex was calmly listening. Then, as my last words vibrate through the air, he sucks in a ragged breath, fists forming, muscles clenching. I watch his reaction, but he gathers himself too quickly, loosens his fists, takes a calming breath, and nods for me to go on. I can't find the strength to finish the sentence. This is too much. Alex envelopes me in his hug, one hand tangled in my hair, the other rubbing my back. I'm sobbing into his chest and can't seem to stop. The floodgates have opened. All the pent-up emotions of my past are surfacing, and I'm drowning in them.

Alex lifts my face to his and kisses my forehead with his gentle lips. My sobs subside for a moment. I realize he is my anchor, my strength, my one true thing. He has not let me down, just supported me and helped me regain my self-confidence. I hold onto him and gain strength to continue.

"This time my dream kept switching between the creep at the beach and Matthew. I woke up feeling powerless and violated, lacking control over my body. That's why I did that to you. I needed to erase the horror and replace it with a beautiful and willful act. And you sensed my need as usual, reigned in your controlling habits, and gave it all up to me. Thank you."

Alex places his hands on my cheeks and kisses my lips gently, rubbing the tips of our noses.

"I've seen the look that was on your face during that nightmare way too many times not to recognize it. I knew you were in pain, mental and physical. So, when you've started the onslaught of wet kisses and frantic touches, I figured you needed to right the balance, gain back the control. We're similar in more ways than you can imagine."

Alex gives me another lingering kiss before prompting me to continue. "I sense you're not done here. Tell me."

As always, he's right on the mark.

"Ever since I came to Miami, I've thought someone's been following me. I've never had that feeling before. It was weird and I was paranoid. I kept feeling eyes on me, but telling myself to chill and not go crazy. Then, last night, I met with my father in Chicago. He confronted me with a set of pictures documenting every day we spent together."

Alex tenses under me, going rigid, his jaw clenching in a struggle to reign control of the building rage. I look into his eyes; they're slowly turning steel grey, the telltale sign of his fury. He nods again and silently prompts me to go on.

"My father claims he received the photos from an anonymous source early in the morning, and had me booked for the next flight that same day. The envelope had a note in it that said *fix this before it becomes public.* I've been given an ultimatum. Forty-eight hours, fix this or lose everything. If the photos go public, besides getting kicked out of the company, I will irrevocably damage my reputation."

I sigh, rip my eyes from the darkness of the ocean, and chance another glance at Alex. He is boiling on the inside, barely keeping calm on the outside. I can't bear seeing his eyes so cold and steely grey. He looks positively murderous right now. It scares me. If not for the gentle embrace of his hands on my back and thighs, I would be running for my life. Our eyes meet again, and his subtle nod prompts me to carry on.

"I'm meeting my father again on Friday. I've tried to explain I left Matthew. The decision has been made. He wants to hear none of that, claiming we are, even now, both cheaters. Friday I'm flying back for a final attempt at opening my father's eyes, making him see the world from my perspective. Hopefully he'll care. I just can't wrap my head around the possibility of becoming sort of a homeless, jobless orphan. I can survive on my own no problem; it's just that life feels like such a waste. Everything I've put my heart and soul into building will be taken away in the blink of an eye."

I take a deep breath, stopping my monologue for a brief moment. My eyes are filled with sincerity, and I'm looking straight at Alex, hoping he sees right through me, as he always does.

"Thank you for being here, for helping me heal, for not leaving, for listening. Thank you for being you."

I kiss the corner of his mouth. My heart swells with emotions. I am so relieved, as if a burden has been lifted from my chest. I feel I can breathe fully for the first time in years. This is me: troubled, complicated, and completely bared to the one person who matters most in my life. Alex kisses my lips gently, pulling away to place his trademark kiss on my forehead. He's silent, expressing his feelings through gentle touches. I'm cradled in his lap, and he relaxes against the chaise. We sit like this in the darkness of the night, warm wind blowing over our tangled bodies. I feel his acceptance of me. But there is something else, a sense of unease that I can't shake away. His rage has subsided a bit. I may not know him that well, but I feel him. I know he's put on a calm mask, but those eyes are still glacial. Hence, I wait patiently, relishing his closeness, calmed by the steady beat of his heart.

Chapter 17

Minutes go by in utter stillness, just the sound of ocean and our beating hearts filling the silence of the warm night. Finally, Alex stirs under me and I lift up from his chest, resuming my position on his lap. Our fingers interlace with a stronger hold, longing for a solid connection. His eyes are haunted, but they are no longer silvery cold. The blues are back, along with unexplainable vulnerability. I dare not say anything. Should he need time, I've got plenty of it.

Alex takes one last, deep breath and starts talking. "Remember when I told you I was not a public person, and that I keep my interactions with women to a minimum? Well, I meant it, every word. I haven't been in a relationship for years. After what happened when I was thirteen, I left the country and lived and studied abroad. I had to protect my identity, for fear of endangering myself, as well as the other person." He looks at me unblinking and I nod, silently telling him I understand.

"One week of your presence has changed my life so much. I can't stay away. The pull is too strong. I crave your closeness, your touch. I crave to protect you, to make love to you, to be with you." I smile at his confession, my heart swelling with emotions, hopes, possibilities. His eyes are trained on mine, but there's pain lingering in them, right alongside infinite tenderness.

"I can't afford to get close to anyone without knowing who they are. It's a mistake that could cost me everything. So not knowing who you were, I had to check. Basically, I knew your name and everything about you the first day I met you. I'm very resourceful in that sense, besides, you had nothing to hide. I had to be certain you weren't connected to my world."

I feel dumbstruck by his admission. I see his reasons, I can even make an argument in favor of his actions, but nonetheless, there's an acrid aftertaste to finding out I was researched, my privacy breached. My lips are tight in a straight line, but that doesn't stop Alex from reading the emotions right off my face. He gets closer to me, our noses almost touching, and pleads with his eyes for me to give him a chance to explain. Then he places a lingering kiss to my forehead.

"One thing was off though. That first day we spent together on the beach I noticed you were followed. That made me even more cautious. It didn't fit in with the rest of your life. You were a good girl on paper, no blips anywhere on the radar. The only explanation that came to my mind was a jealous husband or boyfriend. For your protection, and my peace of mind, I had someone follow you when I wasn't around. And thank god he did. That thug out on the beach had been after you for some time. If you hadn't run away, Vic would have gotten information out of him, but his instructions were clear, your safety is a top priority. He chased you."

My eyes are wide open, mouth slacked. I cannot believe what I'm hearing. After all, I really don't have any idea who Alex is. I thought I was beginning to know him, but he just threw my whole world upside down.

"I will get to the bottom of this. Whoever ordered the shadowing will pay dearly for it. They have no idea what they've gotten themselves into. Those pictures, they will never see the light of the day. I can guarantee you that. Your reputation will not be tarnished; your safety will not be jeopardized. I will not allow our faces to be made public."

Alex looks determined, and I don't doubt him for a second. There must be a good reason he goes to these measures to protect his privacy. I just don't see how I fit in. After all the efforts I've made to have an open, honest relationship, baring my soul, I realize the person in front of me has been doing just the opposite. He has no trust in me. He's caring, understanding, protective, affectionate, tender, supportive, sexy as hell, a perfect combination of gentle and dominant. I realize he is everything I've ever dreamed of in a man. But he doesn't trust me. How can I live with that?
I'm so deep in thought, I lose track of time. Sadness envelopes me, a sense of despair at realizing this is a lose-lose situation. I hate to go, but how can I stay?

A tender hand is on my chin, cueing me to face the man who has pushed me down the rabbit hole I was so desperate to avoid. I turn slowly and see Alex's pained face, the desperation in him palpable.

"Say something. I know you're confused, I never meant for it to come down to this."

"I'm at a loss for words. I don't know where to start. Who are you? I don't even know your last name, or how old you are—all those things that you just took for granted by researching me."

A realization must dawn on him. He clears his throat, straightens his back, and really introduces himself for the first time.

"I am Alexander Faust. I am thirty-six years old. My birthday is April 8th."

My eyes go wide and Alex continues sheepishly, "I know, it's on the same day as yours. I couldn't believe it myself." My heart is beating so fast, ready to jump out of my chest. This is too much. The coincidence is pushing my heart to accept that we were meant to find each other, but my mind is fighting to keep my guard up. Trust is by far the most important building block.

"I can't fathom what else you know about me and how much of it is committed to your memory. You must have been so bored when I was telling you the story of my life. Old news, right?" I'm suddenly bitter over the lost opportunity to get to know each other the normal way. I feel invaded and violated.

"Absolutely not! The information I found was factual and dry; it didn't represent the person you really are. Your spirit, charisma, sense of humor, sexuality, and vulnerability are only known to a few. I'm one of the lucky ones. I can't bear thinking I may have put you in danger. I had no proof who ordered the shadowing. As soon as heard you were in danger, I flew right back to Miami."

"Flew? Where were you? What do you do? Why am I followed by herds of people? Why danger?"

My head is spinning with questions.

"I rent luxury boats to people, different people, ones who need complete privacy for their meetings. We screen them and provide secure arrangements and accommodations for the meetings, as well as staff and security personnel who are trained to keep quiet. Any information about the upcoming meetings or clients is completely confidential. So far there have never been any leaks, and that's why I'm trusted. I deal with people who go above and beyond any laws and civil measures. This is why I had to know exactly who you were. Once I knew you were not part of this business, I had to protect you from it."

He says everything without a pause, then stops for a breath to gauge my reaction. I look him straight in the eye and do not know what to say.

"This is unbelievable; this can't be true. How do you live like this? I see why you had to go to all the measures you did, but in a way, I feel betrayed. You were keeping secrets from me, and looked me straight in the eye without blinking. You knew what happened, yet pretended you didn't, letting me struggle through retelling the horrors."

I'm shaking all over from the onslaught of emotions, suddenly feeling cold in the warm tropical air. Alex places a tentative hand on my cheek, fully expecting I'll flinch from his touch. Surprisingly, I still find it comforting. A lonely tear rolls down and is swiped by his thumb.

"Please don't cry. I can't stand hurting you, knowing I'm the cause of your grief. I swear, I'm ready to move heaven and earth just to make it right with you. I know I betrayed your trust, the most important thing you were looking for in me. Unfortunately, there's still so much more you don't know about me that I'm not ready to share yet. It'll take time for me to reveal all my demons and motivations. They are rooted deep in my history. Please know, I have come clean about everything that concerns you." He still cradles my face in his hand, looking in my eyes, searching them for understanding and perhaps forgiveness.

I crave his touch, the peace it brings. I'm scared to follow my heart.

"I'm not asking for an answer right now. I know you're confused and need to think. I'll give you space. Although the last thing I want to do right now is leave."

The idea of him leaving right now is disturbing. I blurt before I think of the consequences. "Then don't." I stare at him, unable to continue. I'm not making promises. I simply can't let him go.

The understanding passes between us, no words necessary. He needs the physical connection as much as I do. The future is uncertain, the present can be stretched, tomorrow hasn't come yet.

Alex lifts up from the lounger, cradling my tired body in his arms. It dawns on me that I haven't left his lap, haven't broken contact with him the whole time, finding comfort in his closeness, despite being hurt by his words. Our chemistry is unexplainable.

We enter the bedroom and stop. A silent question asked. I tighten my hold on Alex's neck, whispering softly in his ear.

"Let's go to sleep. Tomorrow will be another day." That's all the confirmation he needs. In a few long strides, we climb the mattress and settle in the middle, a perfect tangle of limbs.

Chapter 18

The morning comes too soon. Sun is bright in my face but my body is cold. I know without checking, Alex is gone. This time I don't bother looking for him, knowing it's a waste of time. He won't be here. Tomorrow has come. I wanted space to think, so I got it. Sadly, I don't have any energy left in me to do it. Pulling the blanket over my head, I fall into the oblivion, the rabbit hole consuming me. I welcome the darkness, my new friend in this game of avoidance.

Next time I open my eyes, it's late afternoon. The day is coming to an end, darkness approaching soon. I make myself get up, use the bathroom, brush my teeth. I can't eat, the idea revolting. I grab some water and go to the balcony. Nothing has changed from last night. Except now I'm alone. I lay down on the chaise where Alex sat with me just mere hours ago, my imagination playing tricks on me, causing me to smell his unique scent, a blend of cologne and his natural aroma. I lay on my side, close to the pillow, and watch wave after wave roll over the shore in an endless cycle. The sound is soothing, the warm breeze caressing. I close my eyes and fall, fall, fall down into the darkness.

I wish I could forget everything, at least for a little bit, take a break and feel carefree. The memories attack me even in my sleep.

Images flicker behind my eyes, happy moments, Alex's half smiles, our hands clasped together, his strong shoulders when he carried me from the water, blue eyes darkened with arousal, the gentle touch of his lips to my forehead that always seems to make me feel better. I am in a half-asleep slumber. My heart aches, I miss him terribly, but do I actually miss him, or the image I've created in my mind? I'm so confused, and my trust is so shaken up I no longer know what to believe. Where does the truth end and my imagination begin? I swore to myself I'd never again live under pretenses. Yet here I am, falling for a guy who could write a manual on creating a fake front.

It bothers me that he knew my life history before I had a chance, and choice for that matter, to share it. He probably knows a lot more than he admits. I, on the other hand, know practically nothing about him. What's worse, he admitted he isn't ready to share more, at least not yet. What started as an innocent vacation fling is rapidly evolving into a heartbreak waiting to happen.

I need to pull myself back together. I can't fall deeper or I won't climb out.
I will my body to find strength, get up, and finally do something productive.
This time, once I'm up, I focus on making a list of things that need to be done. I'm flying out first thing tomorrow morning, so I go and repack my bag. As I go around my condo, everything reminds me of our time together. The couch we had sex on, the mirror forever bearing the images of my naked body revealed shamelessly in orgasms, the bed where

Alex let me take control after my nightmare and balance my psyche. The same bed where he pushed me over the edge of ecstasy too many times to count.

This place screams us.

I escape into a hot shower, only to be assaulted by more memories. The first time we stood there, half-dressed and intimate.
I focus on washing my hair and body, unable to block the onslaught of memories.

My hand slides over my breast and I realize my nipples are budded up; I'm aroused. The other hand slides down to the v between my thighs. I touch the gentle folds and find a pool of wetness there. I need to take the edge off; release the pent-up sexual energy I didn't even realize I had.
My fingers slide further between the folds, finding my clit and starting a slow, circular pattern. The coils in my core tighten up even more. I roll my nipples with the free hand, one, then the other, pulling on them slightly, each tug pushing me closer and closer to the peak. I take my time and go very slowly, until I can't physically take it anymore and an orgasm rips through my body, wave after wave, slow circles around my clit prolonging the pleasure and letting me ride it out. I slide down against the wall and sit on the marble shower floor, too spent to move. Water hits my face and shoulders. I pull my knees up and rest my arms and head on top of them, taking a few minutes to regain my senses.

I come out of the shower with renewed strength and the will to deal with what life threw my way. I am determined to take control. At least, that's what I tell myself. Because the more I think about it—the less certain I am that control was ever really mine.

First, I'll go see my father. He needs to know there's no threat behind the pictures. Despite my overall trust issues with Alex, I do trust him fully on this matter. These photos will not see the light of day. It's not only for my protection, but also in his own best interest. In light of recent events, I don't doubt his capabilities. No wonder he had his own key card to enter my condo. How far, exactly, do his capabilities extend? He seems to stop at nothing. And somehow—that should scare me. But it doesn't. Once the fear of public humiliation is put to rest, my father will have to make a decision. Will he stand by my choices, or will he try to bully me into submitting to his ideas? I hope it's not the latter. I am so done with bending to his demands. I fear losing my position in the family business. And yet, part of me hopes I do. Because I've finally felt something close to freedom—and I don't think I would survive losing it a second time.

But the more I learn...the deeper I go. Past the point of control. Past the point of return. Into something I was never meant to see. And now that I have—I can't go back. Because the life I knew is gone. And whatever comes next... I don't know what it is. Only that—there's no going back. And no way out of what's ahead.

This isn't the end. It's the beginning. And I have a feeling—I won't survive it. Not in any way that matters.

Continue in ONE To See Me

From the Author:

Dear Reader,

There's something quietly unsettling about the idea that someone might be watching you... not just noticing, but paying attention. Waiting. Knowing.

This story began with a question that stayed with me:
How much of what we believe about our lives is actually true?

Emmeline thinks she knows her world. She trusts what she sees, what she feels, what she's been told. But as things begin to shift, so does her sense of reality—and the deeper she looks, the harder it becomes to separate truth from illusion.

This is a story about trust, perception, and the things we don't question until we have no choice. About the fragile line between safety and control.

If you found yourself questioning everything, turning pages faster than you meant to...
then you were right where I hoped you'd be.

Thank you for being here.

— Alicia

Welcome to the ONE World—where every story reveals something new... and nothing is ever as simple as it seems.

Acknowledgements:

To the readers—

Thank you for taking a chance on this story, for turning the pages, and for stepping into this world with me. Your time, your curiosity, and your willingness to feel something through these characters mean more than I can put into words.

And to those who continue this journey from one book to the next...
thank you for staying.

— Alicia

Stay Connected:

www.AliciaMaxwell.com

Alicia@AliciaMaxwell.com

www.facebook.com/AliciaMaxwellAuthor

www.instagram.com/alicia_maxwell_author

http://www.subscribepage.com/AliciaMaxwell

http://www.subscribepage.com/Alicia_Maxwell_New Release